Trio in Death-Sharp Minor

A Justinia Wright Private Investigator Mystery

CW Hawes

CWH Books

Join the Team!

I invite you to become a VIP Reader. You'll get a free copy of *Vampire House and other early cases of Justinia Wright, P.I.* right off the bat.

Then each month, maybe more often, you'll get a variety of good things to keep you up to date with my many worlds, as well as curated content.

Just click, tap, or scan the QR code to begin the adventure!

Cover art by Raihana Dewji

This one is for Jodi.

Contents

Love Out Of Death

1 – Monday, 3 March

"Did you see this?" I asked.

Tina and I were at breakfast. She was reading her iPad and occasionally taking a sip of tea or a bite of toast. She's not a morning person and prefers a Spartan breakfast. I'm about fifty-fifty, starting off some days with a continental and others with a full monty. This morning it was a continental with two soft-boiled eggs.

Without looking at me, she said, "See what?"

Manley meowed loudly for his morning treat.

"They found the body of Alicia Harris."

"Who?"

"Alicia Harris. Heiress to the Harris millions. A lesbian on the QT, but one of the first to get married. Avid sportswoman. Patron of the art museum and the Guthrie."

"Was she pretty?"

"Not especially so. On the plain side. Makeup a plus."

"Your kind of woman."

That comment I ignored.

"Pulled her out of Wirth Lake yesterday afternoon. Had been ice fishing."

"With whom?"

"Mostly people from Harris Industries."

"Were they actually fishing or just partying?"

"Don't know."

"Foul play?"

"Doesn't say."

She took a sip of tea and wrinkled her nose.

"Let me get you a fresh cup. It's hotter if you drink it right away."

She waved her hand in the air as if dismissing a menial servant. I may be her servant, but I'm not menial. No Man Friday or Majordomo of the Wright household is menial. I got up and went to the kitchen, poured ourselves fresh cups of tea, and snared myself another turnover. I'd already eaten the ones on the plate in the dining room.

I gave her back her teacup, filled with hot tea.

"You could've brought me one." Her eyes taking in my turnover.

I gave it to her and returned to the kitchen for another. Back at the table, I drank tea and took a bite of the pastry.

"Was the hife with her?"

"The what?"

"The hife. Husband. Wife. Hife."

"Did you make that up?"

"I don't know. Might have."

"No. The spouse's brother was, though. Apparently he works for Harris Industries."

"What capacity?"

"Don't know. Paper didn't say."

"What's his name?"

"Greg Pinneman."

She looked at me. I spelled the last name. She tapped on the iPad. "He's Director of Market Research. What's the hife's name?"

"Let me see. Nope. The article doesn't mention it. If I recall I think it's Beatrice."

She looked at me. "Are you serious?"

"I think that's her name."

"How old is she?"

"Forties, I think."

"Who the hell would name their kid *Beatrice* in this day and age?"

"Her parents. Maybe they were into opera."

Tina glowered at me, shook her head, and drank tea.

Her silence indicated we were done discussing the death of Alicia Harris. Someone naming their kid Beatrice was too much for Tina to handle at 8:35 on a Monday morning. Having looked at whatever the iPad had to offer, she finished her tea and turnover, and got up from the table.

"Office?" I said.

She nodded and left.

I finished reading the paper and eating my breakfast, then cleaned up the dishes.

Business has been slow. The long, cold, snowy winter must've also put a damper on that part of human nature which ends up requiring the services of a private investigator. Spring will be here soon and with it, hopefully, some business. Otherwise I'd have to start chasing ambulances to drum up some cash to prevent my paycheck from bouncing. Unless Tina decided to sell the paintings she's done since the doldrums hit. Four copies of Michael Kungl art deco prints. The originals are very cool and Tina's copies are, well, very difficult to not take for the real thing.

Dishes taken care of and food put away, I went to the office. The air was heavy with cigar smoke. I cracked a couple windows and started a fan to push the airborne remnants of the Muniemaker Long to the outside world and bring in some early March air that was marginally more breathable.

Living in a city one never has truly fresh, unpolluted air with which to fill the lungs. But one makes do. Of course she'd call me a hypocrite if I were to light up my pipe. And I suppose I would be.

I looked over the bank account. We still had money in it. I dusted the room. Tina turned a page in her book, took a sip of madeira, and lit a fresh cigar. I went out to the kitchen and checked what was available for lunch and supper. We had food. We wouldn't starve. I went back to the office and sat at my desk. I picked up the book on surveillance techniques I was a third of the way into and began reading.

Tina looked up from her book. "You heard anything from Tatty?"

Tatiana Bogar is a chess buddy who was studying geology at the U last year. We became somewhat intimate and then she went home for Christmas and reconnected with her boyfriend and transferred to the University of Budapest.

"Other than the tournament we were just in, no. She's been pretty quiet. I suppose Lazlo, well, you know."

Tina nodded. "She's a nice gal. I miss seeing her."

"Yeah, me too."

The doorbell rang. Ten to ten. I put the book down and went to the door.

On the porch was our good friend Cal Swenson, a lieutenant with the Minneapolis police department's homicide unit. In addition to being our friend, he is my sister's occasional lover. At the moment they're more friends than lovers. But the situation was the same last year and suddenly they got all hot and heavy. So who knows?

"Hi, Major. Is the Red Baron in?"

"Hi, Cal. She is. Come on in."

Cal often calls me *Major*, short for Majordomo. He refers to Tina as the *Red Baron* or the *General*. The former because of her flaming red hair and the aristocratic manner she frequently displays; the latter, due to how she takes charge of a case. He came in and went into the office, with me in his wake.

"The Major said you were in."

Tina looked up from her book and closed it on a finger. "Hi there, Sweet Cheeks. Have a seat."

Cal sat in the oversized oxblood leather wingback, which isn't oversized for him. I went to my desk.

"Got a case. Just got it, in fact, and the family's already screaming for it to be solved yesterday."

Cal must be in a hurry. No chitchat.

"Alicia Harris," Tina said.

Surprise flitted across his face, then he smiled. "The Major primed your pump." He cast me a we-guys-have-to-stick-together grin.

Tina puffed on her cigar.

He leaned back in his chair. I guess he wasn't in such a hurry after all. "You know, Buttercup, those things will kill you."

"And so will life. You here to consult or insult your best resource?"

"My, my. You get out of the wrong side of bed or wasn't he that good?"

"Better than you."

"Really now. It's been so long maybe we should have a rerun to check your memory."

Tina laughed out loud. "Now that's some pickup line. Okay, Swenson, what do you want?"

"You."

"Professionally or...?"

"Both."

Tina smiled. "Business before pleasure. What do you have?"

"Alicia Harris. Pulled out of Wirth Lake. Stabbed twice in the heart with an ice pick."

"Interesting choice of weapon."

"That it is. Murderer has a sense of humor."

"Bring the file?"

"I have it. Want to look at it over lunch?"

A big smile appeared on her face. "Now that is a hook I'll bite at."

"See, Major. Offer her food and you can reel her in."

"Oh, cut the crap Swenson. I'm letting you buy me lunch. I didn't say you could screw me for dessert."

"I thought we're friends with benefits?"

"We are. Your benefit today is you get to treat me to lunch."

I cut in. "Cal, you better stop before you find out you're using a backhoe."

"Don't I know it," he replied.

Tina looked at the clock on her desk. "Ten-thirty is a little early for lunch."

"It is," Swenson replied. "I have some new music I want you to listen to."

"Not more Jonathan Colton."

"No."

"Okay, big spender, where we going?"

"Mac's."

"Always knew there was a fishy side to you."

I groaned. "Good God, Tina, that was bad." For those of you who don't know, Mac's is a fish and chips shop.

Cal pinched his nose. "Geez, Wright."

Tina just smiled, sashayed around her desk, and on out the door. Cal got up and followed.

Tina poked her head back in. "Oh, Harry, the usual."

"Gotcha," I replied.

Those two took off and I set about my task, which was to find out all I could on Alicia Harris while they were out and about. Better than any paper trail is the internet trail people leave behind. And that's where my shovel was going first.

By quarter to one, my eyes were blurry. I went to the kitchen and looked in the fridge. Plenty of food, but I was in the mood for something on the greasy side with cheese. I grabbed my car keys, coat, and hat, locked up the place, got in my car, and headed north. Driving across downtown and into Northeast Minneapolis, I pulled into White Castle.

The clerk at the counter, Ann, greeted me by name. I ordered ten double bacon cheese sliders, a large fry, an onion ring, and got a glass for water. I hate pop, save for birch beer or cream soda. When my food was ready, I took it out to my car to eat. I put on some music and thought about Alicia Penelope Harris, age fifty, daughter and only child of the late Benjamin James Harris and his equally late wife, Elise Moreen Harris (nee Merton). Eating sliders and listening to Bantock helps me sort out the data.

Old Man Harris had four disappointments in life: Alicia was a daughter, she was a lesbian, had no interest in running Harris Industries, and he couldn't get his golf game lower than eight over par. And not necessarily in that order.

His greatest joy was flying. Said joy ended when he flew the company jet into a mountain killing himself, his wife, and two friends fifteen years ago.

Alicia quietly came out of the closet publicly one Christmas ten years ago. Two years later she left her partner of four years and took up with Beatrice Pinneman, known to everyone as Bea. The two got married six and a half months ago, just after it became legal in Minnesota. The Harris fortune will probably pass to Bea. A possible incentive for murder. Alicia met Bea at a company party to which she'd been invited by her brother, Greg.

Two years ago Alicia started taking an interest in running Harris Industries. Walford Richards, current board chairman and CEO, and longtime friend of the late Ben Harris, has quarreled publicly with Alicia concerning the company's future. There was speculation she might try to oust Richards at the upcoming stockholder's meeting. Being dead means she probably won't pursue Richards's ouster, which could be motive for him to have found a way to stick an ice pick in her heart.

The internet is good, but it has limits. Tina will still have to talk to people and I'll probably have to find some paper along the way. I finished my last slider. The French fries and onion rings were already gone. I think they are best really hot, so I eat them first. With my food all gone and the car clock telling me the time was 1:58, the time had arrived to head home and see what Tina found out.

Traffic was something else. I parked in front of the house at 2:43. Swenson was just leaving. I got out of the car. He waved and I waved back. As sure as there's snow in Minneapolis in the winter, they decided to have dessert at home.

I unlocked the door, hung up my coat, and went to the office. Tina was there, sitting behind her desk, smoking a cigar.

"How was lunch?" I asked

"It was fine."

"How was dessert?"

"Satisfying."

"Why don't you two just get married? You act like you've been married for twenty years."

She ignored my comment and asked, "Did you find anything?"

"I did." And I proceeded to tell her what I'd discovered.

"Interesting. Autopsy report came back this morning, confirming she was murdered. Probably sometime after the party ended at eleven. Police are working on getting a list of suspects. The usual police routine. They got a statement from the hife when she identified the body. I want to start with her. Then talk to Walford Richards."

"Okay."

"See if you can get Walford here tomorrow. We'll go see the spouse now."

▼

The Harris home wasn't far from us. Several years ago, Alicia sold her parents's house in North Oaks, then bought and renovated an old mansion by the art institute. We rang the doorbell. A woman answered the door, asking if she could help us.

"We're here to see Bea Pinneman. Police business," I said.

The woman hesitated, then invited us in and asked us to wait in the foyer. She came back in a couple of minutes and said Ms. Pinneman would see us in the drawing room. The woman led the way and showed us in.

Bea is a willowy woman. Everything about her seems fragile. She greeted us with a quiet voice and invited us to sit. We introduced ourselves.

Tina said, "I want to be clear. We are not the police. We are consultants to the police."

"I see," Bea said in a soft and rather high-pitched voice. "So I don't have to talk to you."

"If you don't," Tina continued, "we'll be back with the police and ask our questions then."

"I see. Well, I suppose it makes no difference."

"Do you mind if I record our conversation?" I asked. "My shorthand isn't the best."

Bea smiled, a very pretty smile. "If you must. I don't really have much to say. I already gave a statement to the police."

"I know," Tina said. "I read it. But that was a sheet of paper."

"Okay. What would you like to know?"

"How long were you and Alicia together?" Tina asked.

"Eight years. We were married in August."

"Did you not have a ring?"

Bea blushed. "I... I took it off when I found out."

"Found out?" Tina asked.

"That Alicia died," Bea said.

"Why's that?" Tina continued.

"Well, uh, you see... Oh, God..."

Tina and I said nothing, letting Bea work through whatever she was working through. She stopped, took a deep breath, and then continued. "Well, Ms. Wright—What? Did I say something?"

My sister had wrinkled her nose when Bea called her Ms. Wright.

I explained, "Miss Wright. 'MS' is the abbreviation for manuscript."

Bea's face was a blank, then she started giggling. "Oh. I get it."

Tina smiled to show all was forgiven. "You were going to say why you took off your wedding ring."

In a second, Bea's lightheartedness vanished. She was once again under the weight of years. "I didn't love her. Not any more. I don't know why I agreed to get married.

But because I did, I am very rich and now Greg won't lose his job."

"Greg's your brother?"

Bea nodded.

"Was he going to lose his job?"

"If Alicia got control of the company, yes."

"Even though he was your brother?"

She nodded. "Alicia could be very cold and heartless and..."

"She abused you, didn't she?" Tina asked.

Bea bit her lip.

"She hit you?" Tina pressed.

"Only once. When Greg found out, he threatened to kill her. Not that he would. You know how people say things. And a couple of years ago at a company get together he had too much to drink. He saw Alicia grab my arm and he started screaming at her. Alicia demanded Walford fire him, but Walford just laughed at her. I think that's when she decided to take back control of the company."

"Just to get your brother fired?"

"And to get rid of Walford. She hated Walford."

"Why?"

"She said he groped her when she was a kid. I don't know if it's true. Walford and Alicia's father were best of friends. Alicia could be a drama queen. She might have said that just to get attention or get back at her father."

Tina paused. She tented her fingers and rested her chin on them. Bea looked at her, then looked at me. I smiled. She smiled back. Yes, indeed, a very beautiful smile. Then she looked at her hands. Finally Tina asked, "What are you going to do with the money?"

"I don't know. I don't want it. Really, I don't. I don't want to own forty percent of Harris Industries either."

"Alicia have a will?"

"Yes. I have a copy. I get everything."

"You going to give the money away?"

"I don't know. Maybe. You see, Miss Wright, my brother and I, well, we come from simple working backgrounds. He wants me to keep the money. But I really don't want it. I just want to be happy. I want someone to love me for who I am and not how much I'm worth."

"You were married before?"

"Yes. I was twenty-five. Phil was a short man and angry and abusive. He used to hit me until Greg found out and beat him up. Broke his arm. A year later we got a divorce. Five years of hell. No children. I dated some. Eventually took up with Alicia. A real change. I thought maybe a woman would be more caring. But she was cruel. Not at first. It developed slowly. It would have been better if she hit me."

"I'm sorry," Tina said.

Bea nodded.

"Do you have any thoughts on who might want Alicia dead?"

"You mean aside from me? No. Not really. I wanted her dead, Miss Wright, but I never thought she would end up dead. I used to wish a bus would hit her or something. You know?"

Tina nodded.

Bea let out a short, brittle, bitter laugh. "Now she is dead and I have all her money and all I wanted was for her to love me."

I stood and moved next to Bea. "Here's our card."

Tina stood. "Call me if you think of anything else. We'll pass this on to the police."

We left and driving home Tina said nothing. She parked the car in the garage and we entered the house.

"You know, Harry, she's one messed up person."

"I don't think so. She wants what we all want. To be loved. She's just not looking in the right places and doesn't get out of a bad situation fast enough."

II – Tuesday, 4 March

WALFORD RICHARDS WAS SEVEN minutes late for his eleven-fifteen appointment. He blamed the traffic.

"You say you're working for the police?"

"Yes," Tina replied.

"You have proof?"

"Lieutenant Cal Swenson will verify."

"Why isn't he here?"

"He should be," Tina said and added, "He must've gotten hung up in traffic."

Richards gave her a sideways look, probably wondering if she was tweaking him.

"Do you want to wait for Lieutenant Swenson?"

"No, no. Let's get this over with. I'll verify later and if he doesn't corroborate, I sue you. How's that?"

Tina was pissed. "No need to be nasty, Mr. Richards. In fact, I think it best if we wait for Lieutenant Swenson."

I stepped out of the office and called Cal. We hadn't planned on him being at the meeting, so I wasn't sure I'd get him but he picked up on the third ring.

"Hey, Major. How can I help you?"

I explained the situation. He laughed. "The General needs the cavalry's assistance. Okay, I'll be there in ten."

I returned to the office and said Swenson should be arriving in ten minutes.

"Let's get on with it then," Richards said.

"No. I don't care to be sued. We'll wait."

"For Christ's sake, Ms. Wright." Now Richards would need Christ. He looked at me. I shrugged. He looked at Tina. She looked back. "Fine," he said, "we wait."

Ten minutes of quiet was interrupted by the doorbell. I let Cal in and walked with him into the office. He introduced himself to Richards and apologized for being late. After Cal got seated, Tina began.

"Where were you, Mr. Richards, on the night of Friday, the twenty-eighth of February?" Tina asked.

"I was at home with my wife. We watched a movie together."

"How concerned were you about being forced out of the company?"

"Not very. Alicia was trying to stir up trouble but she hadn't gotten very far. My leadership has made the stockholders money and that's what they care about in the end."

"If she did gain control of the company and forced you out, what would you do?"

"Look, Ms. Wright— What did I say?"

Tina's face looked like she was chewing a lemon.

"Miss Wright," I said.

"Huh?" Apparently Richards was hard of hearing.

"Not Ms. It's Miss Wright."

"Really? Okay. I'm sorry, uh, Miss Wright. I'm well set. Aside from my share of the company, I'm worth at least three hundred million dollars. I'm sixty-seven. I'll survive quite well should I lose my job."

"Why do you think someone would want to kill Alicia?"

"I don't know. She was a rather nasty person behind the scenes. Pleasant and charming in public. I heard she was stepping out on Bea. Don't know if that is true. But the rumor was flying around."

"How many ice picks do you own, Mr. Richards?"

Richards laughed. "What kind of question is that? I don't think I own any. Not in this day and age. I have an ice cube maker, Miss Wright."

"Thank you for your time, Mr. Richards."

Cal said, "Harry, I'll want a copy."

"Sure thing," I replied. "A call is coming in," I announced. "Cal, would you see Mr. Richards out?"

He nodded and I took the call, "Wright Investigations."

"Hello," the voice said, "this is Bea Pinneman. Is this Mr. Wright?"

"It is, Ms. Pinneman."

"Uh, hi, how are you?"

"I'm fine. Yourself?"

"Well, uh, I'm, I guess fine. Um, could I talk to you?"

"We're doing that now."

She let out a laugh. "I guess we are. I mean, may I see you in person?"

I wasn't sure what she was driving at. "Sure, Ms. Pinneman, we can come to your place or you can come here."

"I'm, uh, I'm not being too clear am I?"

"No. You aren't."

I heard her take a deep breath. "Mr. Wright, would you meet me at the art institute?"

"Just me?"

"Yes. Just you."

"Okay. When?"

"Now."

"Okay. I'm on my way."

"Thank you, Mr. Wright."

She ended the call. Tina was looking at me questioningly.

"That was Bea Pinneman. She wants me to meet her at the art institute."

Tina raised her eyebrows in surprise. Then a smirk appeared on her face. "Tell me how it goes."

▼

Twenty-one blocks. That's how far the Minneapolis Institute of Arts is from Tina's house. The drive took no time at all. Bea was waiting. She smiled and extended her hand. When I took it to shake hands, she pulled me in for a quick hug.

"Thank you for seeing me, Mr. Wright."

"No problem. How can I help you, Ms. Pinneman?"

"You mind if we walk around? And, please, call me Bea."

"Alright, Bea. Call me Harry. Sure. Let's see the sights."

We walked up to the second floor and started with the Japanese collections.

"Harry, don't be mad at me."

"Okay. I won't."

"I didn't tell you everything."

"Most people don't."

"Really? I mean you're a detective and all."

"I'm not a detective. Well, I have a license. My sister is the real detective."

"I see. Well, I'd rather talk to you. You're kind and gentle. Your sister reminds me of Alicia."

I'd have to remember that so I could tweak Tina with it at the appropriate time. I said, "Okay. Talk to me."

We stood before the tea house. She reached over and took my hand.

"I suspected Alicia was seeing someone, so I hired a detective to find out who. She was seeing Melody Johnson."

The name was familiar, but I couldn't place it.

"Who's Melody Johnson?"

"She owns eighteen percent of Harris Industries. If she and Alicia teamed up, they'd control fifty-eight percent."

Now the name rang a bell. "So the detective got proof Alicia was cheating on you?"

"Yes, he did."

"Did you confront Alicia?"

"No, I didn't."

"Why not?"

"I wanted to wait and see what happened."

"And now it doesn't matter." I watched her reactions.

"No. Not really. Not anymore. I'm a free woman." She squeezed my hand, then let go. "Are you married, Harry?"

"No. I was, though."

"Are you glad you're free?"

An interesting question that. I wasn't sure how to answer it. I said, "I don't know if 'glad' is quite the right word. At the time, I'd say 'relieved' was a better choice. And perhaps 'disappointed'. Now? Water under the bridge."

"Well, I'm glad I'm free. Free of Alicia, that is."

The pottery was interesting, but she more so. No grief. I looked at her. She turned and met my gaze.

"You must think I'm terrible. But I'm not sad she's gone. She was a wicked person. I'm glad to be free of her."

She put her arms around me and laid her head on my shoulder. The sobs were soft and gentle. I put my arms around her and held her. So thin and fragile. Like a net of glass filaments.

"I'm sorry, Harry. I've gotten your coat wet."

"You okay?"

She nodded, took a deep breath, and exhaled. "I haven't had lunch. Would you mind having lunch with me?"

"Not at all."

She insisted on driving. Because she'd walked to the museum, we walked to her place to get her car. When she got into a bright yellow Fiat 500 I was very surprised.

"I'm not into cars. That was Alicia's thing. She has a Jaguar and a Maserati. This gets me where I need to go."

We didn't go anywhere fancy for lunch either, but Quangs has the best Vietnamese food this side of Vietnam. We ordered pho. It's to die for.

We talked about all manner of things and I found myself liking Bea very much. She's a simple person. Doesn't want much out of life. Doesn't expect much. When we were done she insisted on paying. When I protested, she laughed and said, "Harry what is twenty dollars to me? I have over nine hundred million. Please. This is my treat. You can pay when I've given it all away." I laughed and said she had a deal.

She dropped me off at my car. Before I got out of her bright yellow Fiat, she leaned over and kissed me. She touched my cheek. "Does it bother you I was with a woman?"

I said, "No." After a pause, I asked, "Are you sure you want to be kissing me?"

She leaned over and kissed me again, for a long time. When we came up for air, she said, "I'm sure."

"Thanks, Bea, for the info, lunch, and a wonderful afternoon."

"Call me?"

"I'll call."

"Thanks, Harry."

I closed the door, got into my old Focus wagon. She drove off and I drove home.

I opened the door and heard music. Tina was in the music room playing Liszt's piano transcription of Beethoven's seventh symphony. I made my way to the room and stood just inside the door. When she saw me, she paused. I told her everything, knowing full well she'd give me crap about what happened. And she did. But she thanked me. She said the afternoon's events were enlightening.

"So when should I start looking for a new assistant?" she asked.

"You trying to get rid of me?"

"Obviously she's fallen head over heels for you or she's trying to manipulate you. Could be both I suppose."

"Could be."

"Don't you think she's a bit skinny for you?"

"Look. She gave me a full court press. It was nice. But I don't think it will last. People in grief do a lot of funny things."

"She isn't. That's the very interesting thing, Harry. She's not grieving. You yourself said as much. She truly wanted the hife dead. The question before us is, did she do it or hire someone who did or worked with someone who did?"

"Like her brother."

"Precisely."

"I don't know, Tina. I don't think she's the type to kill someone. What she wants more than anything is for someone to love her and appreciate her."

"You nearly had me convinced of that, but now...? She hardly knows you and she's sticking her tongue in your mouth."

"She did not."

"Says you." She got up and we walked into the office. Isis following us. When I sat down, the cat jumped into my lap, and curled up. "She must be cold," I said. Isis is a sphinx, one of those hairless cats. Pretty soon in strutted Manley, followed by Prudy.

Tina sat at her desk and poured a glass of madeira and lit a cigar. "Harry, it's not ethical for you to be intimate with one of the suspects."

"I know."

"But don't discourage her."

"But what if I want to?"

She frowned. "I can't make you do anything. Just a request. I want to see what she does or doesn't ask of you."

"I'll think about it."

"Thank you."

I set Isis on the floor and went to the kitchen to make tea. This was certainly an interesting afternoon. The willowy brunette Bea Pinneman putting the make on me. Is it because I just happened to be there? Or is she trying to manipulate me? I honestly don't think she's trying to manipulate me. I think she's lonely. Been lonely most of her forty-seven years. But what if her brother, seeing how miserable she is, decided to relieve her misery and make sure he had a job all at the same time? Now that seemed a likely scenario. But the investigation was early.

The doorbell rang. I looked at the microwave clock. Quarter past five. I went to the door and looked out the peephole. Bea. What does she want?

I opened the door. "Hi, Bea."

"Hi, Harry."

"What brings you here?"

She pointed back towards the street. There was a Maserati GranTurismo parked in front of the house. Only it wasn't any old GranTurismo. It was an MC Stradale. In cherry red.

"Okay. You came here in a Maserati."

She laughed. "That's *why* I'm here, too. I want you to have it."

"Uh, come on in."

She came in and I closed the door. Tina came out of the office.

"Hello, Miss Wright."

"Hello, Ms. Pinneman."

Tina touched my arm and went on down the hall towards the living room.

"Uh, Bea, I really appreciate your thoughtfulness. But I can't accept the car. It's a conflict of interest. We're working for the police. It's like you bribing a police officer."

"Oh, dear. I hadn't thought of that. Oh, my, Harry. This afternoon. I'm... Please don't think..." She sat on the deacon's bench we have in the foyer. "Harry, I really like you. Please don't think I'm trying to bribe you. I have nothing to hide. I wanted to be out of a bad situation. I even wished she'd die. But I didn't kill her. I didn't. But I'm glad she's gone. And you're so kind and gentle. I think you really are and, well, I, I just want to know what that's like."

I sat next to her. "Bea, thanks for the vote of confidence. For now, though, we're going to have to leave this where it is and maybe come back to it later. Okay?"

She nodded.

"I'm interested and you're interested. If we're still interested when this is over, we'll pick it up then. Okay?"

"Sure, Harry. I'd like that. I'm sorry. Please don't think badly of me."

"I don't."

She kissed me. It was passionate and steamy. Who'd think it of a rather plain and simple woman?

"Don't forget me. And you'll call me when this is over?"

"I'll call you, Bea. I promise."

She touched my cheek, then stood up. I walked her out to the car, said goodnight, and she drove off. I walked back to the house. Tina was waiting for me in the foyer. Her look expecting me to spill the beans.

"Bea wanted to give me Alicia's Maserati GranTurismo MC Stradale."

Tina's eyes grew big. "Holy shit. She has it bad."

"In cherry red." I had to toss that in. Red being Tina's favorite color.

"Harry, do you like her?"

We walked back to the living room. A fire was burning in the fireplace. Tina sat in her rocker recliner. I sat in my rocking chair.

"Yes, I do. She's forty-seven going on twelve, but I like her. She has a simple, naive view of life. She just wants someone to love her and be kind to her. Kind of what we all want, isn't it?"

Tina nodded. "It is."

"I know what you're thinking," I said.

"You do?"

"You're willing to take me off the case so I can pursue Bea. Actually let Bea pursue me."

Tina smirked. "She might be just the thing for you, Harry."

"Ha. A famous person once told me, 'Physician, heal thyself.' No. Let's let it sit. I want to be sure a murderess isn't after me."

Tina lit a fresh cigar and refreshed her glass of madeira. "Okay. Call Gwen in the morning, will you? If she's available, I have some work for her."

"Cal won't like the extra expense."

"Too bad. I need an unknown to do some work on the case. Also see if Cal will arrange a meeting with Greg Pinneman."

"Sure thing."

We sat there for awhile, until Tina decided to go out to get something to eat. She asked if I wanted to go with her, but I declined. After she left, I realized the pho had long since gone its way and I was hungry. I went to the kitchen and realized Bea had interrupted my tea preparations. I made tea and then looked at what I could have for supper. Nothing interested me, although there was a lot to be interested in. I decided on White Castle. Tea made. I had a cup. Then filled a thermos and headed out the door.

III – Wednesday, 5 March

I CALLED GWEN POISSON at seven and got her. Probably still in bed. I asked if she was available and she said maybe. Depended on what Tina wanted. I told her to stop by and Tina would explain. She said she would. At eight I got hold of Swenson and he said we had good timing. He was scheduled to meet with Pinneman at eleven in his office. I told him we'd be there.

Breakfast was ready when Tina came downstairs at eight-thirty. Isis was wound around her neck like a scarf. I said good morning. Tina muttered something that might have been good morning and sat at the table. I brought in tea, toast, fresh fruit, cream, and a selection of pastries.

"We have a meeting with Pinneman at eleven in his office," I informed her. "Swenson had already set it up. Gwen said she'd be here sometime this morning."

She nodded. Her nose stuck in her iPad checking on whatever it is she checks on in the morning.

I unfolded the paper and my eye caught the painting hanging on the wall facing me: *After Shishkin's 'Brook in Birch Forest'*. I've worked for Tina for several years now and I still find her working as a private eye incongruous with her talents. And might I add her artistic personality. I shook my head and began reading the paper. I was reading a story on page three when the doorbell rang. I put the paper down and got up to answer it. On the doorstep was Gwen. I invited her in.

"Hi Gwen. Long time no see. Your hair is coming in nicely." In a rather grisly adventure last year, Gwen was kidnapped and had her head shaved.

She gave me a hug. "It has been. Good to see you, Harry. And thanks."

"Tina's eating. Have some breakfast with us."

"Sounds good."

We walked to the dining room.

"Morning, Tina," Gwen said.

"Morning," the great detective replied. "Eat something. Your hair is looking better all the time."

"Thanks!" Gwen said.

"Make sure Harry washes his hands. He's been reading the paper."

Gwen said, "Yeah, Harry, wash your hands."

"You know, that isn't even worthy of response," I shot back. Gwen laughed and Tina smiled.

I know Gwen doesn't care for coffee or tea or anything with caffeine. Juice, tisanes, and cucumber-infused water are her beverages of choice. I got orange juice and poured her a glass.

"Thanks, Harry," Gwen said. She took a drink, spooned fruit into a bowl, and asked Tina, "What do you have for me?"

Tina said, "I want you to do surveillance."

"Day or night?"

"Day." Tina looked around for pencil and paper. Spied my notebook, reached across the table, and took it along with my pencil. She wrote down an address. "I want to know who comes out and when and who goes in and when."

She passed the sheet of paper to Gwen, who took a look and said, "Simple enough. This is the Harris residence, right?"

Tina nodded.

"I can swing it," Gwen said.

"Good," Tina replied. "Harry, give Gwen some cash."

I went to the office, opened the safe, and took out two hundred dollars in small bills. Wrote the amount in the ledger, then locked the safe. I returned to the dining room and gave Gwen the cash. I noticed the fruit and juice were gone.

"Best be going," Gwen said. "Thanks for the job, Tina."

"Don't mention it," she replied. "Take some fruit and pastries with you. Harry, get Gwen a bag."

"No pastries, Harry. I don't do sugar," Gwen reminded me.

Tina said, "Sorry, Gwen, I forgot."

"Not a prob."

Gwen took an apple, a pear, and a bunch of grapes. "Thanks, guys. Catch you later. I'll see my way out, Harry."

"Bye Gwen," I said. When she'd left, I said to Tina, "So you decided to spy on my new friend."

"Just making sure everything is on the up and up."

"No problem. It's what we do."

"The sooner we get her cleared, the sooner you two can get on with your torrid romance and burn up the bedsheets."

"Tell me, is sex all you think about?"

"No. You know that."

"I do?"

Tina transferred her gaze from iPad to my face. "I think about food and painting and music and madeira and cigars and my cats and you. Want me to go on?"

"No. I guess you do think about a few things other than getting laid."

She rolled her eyes. "The thanks I get for trying to help you out."

"Sorry. Don't mean to be unappreciative."

I picked up the paper and she went back to her iPad. At ten fifteen we walked out to the garage, got into Tina's Crossfire, and took off for downtown. Harris Industries' corporate headquarters occupies two floors of the Rand Tower, the third and the twenty-fifth. Our quarry's office was on the twenty-fifth floor. Apparently the grunts were on the third. Tina parked in a ramp. We hoofed it to our destination and got there with a minute to spare. Cal was waiting.

"Morning, Wright. Major. I already let his secretary know we were here."

We sat and waited. Ten minutes later we were ushered into Pinneman's office. We meeted and greeted, exchanged small talk, and then Cal began asking questions. The usual police stuff. When he was done, he asked Tina if she had any questions.

"Do your co-workers see you as hot-headed, Mr. Pinneman?" she asked.

He laughed. "I suppose they do, because, well, I often am. But I'm fair. No one can accuse me of not being fair."

"You broke your ex-brother-in-law's arm and you threatened to kill Alicia Harris. Why should we believe you didn't?"

"Because I didn't."

"Hire someone to do it?"

"Didn't do that either. Look, Ms. Wright, I do what I can to protect Bea. But she makes bad relationship choices. I might try to scare someone, but I wouldn't kill anyone. I have a family. I'm not going to prison for Bea."

"But it seems you have a temper. Maybe that ice pick got stuck into Alicia Harris by accident." Pinneman was shaking his head. Tina went on, "Maybe in a fit of rage your threat didn't remain a threat."

"Nope. Never happened. Never will. Like I said, I'm not going to prison for Bea. She's my sister and I love her, but my family comes first."

"Very well, Mr. Pinneman. Thank you for your time."

The three of us left Pinneman's office and, upon reaching the street, parted company with Cal. Tina and I walked to the ramp, got into the Chrysler, and drove on home.

For our supper I made Cream of Barley Soup; Acorn Squash stuffed with raisins, dried figs, and hazelnuts; and Tofu Chili.

When Tina saw the food set out on the dining room table she wrinkled her nose.

I put my hands on my hips and said, "What's the matter?"

She shook her head and sat down. "Sure wish you'd get off this vegetarian kick. God. You're getting as bad as Gwen."

"It's just better—"

"Yeah, I know. Don't eat it if it has the three Bs. God."

For those of you who don't know, the three Bs are breath, brains, and blood. We were finishing supper when the phone rang. I looked at the name. "Gwen," I said. Tina nodded. "Hey, Gwen. What do you have for us?"

"Nothing much. Bea Pinneman was out from one to three."

"She drive or walk?" I asked.

"Walked. At two-thirty, a package was delivered. That's it. I'm calling it a day."

"Thanks, Gwen. Oh, and Tina won't admit it, but she likes your Tofu Chili."

"Great! We'll make a vegetarian out of her yet."

I relayed the information to Tina.

"Shit. Me? A vegetarian?" She shuddered. "I want you to call Bea and find out what you can about her servant."

"Now?"

"After supper is fine. Better yet, meet her someplace."

"Okay. Any particular reason?"

"No. But just in case the butler did it, we should find out about her."

"Sure thing."

"Oh, you care to tell me how White Castle gets around the Three Bs?"

She had me there. "I'm an ovo-lacto-carno vegetarian."

She rolled her eyes and shook her head. Then said, "Yeah, me too. Especially the carno part."

Tina finished her bowl of chili, while I finished my stuffed squash. When we were done eating, I cleared the table while Tina finished her glass of wine. With the dishes in the dishwasher and the leftovers put away, I called Bea's number.

"Harry! What a surprise! How are you?"

"I'm fine, Bea. You?"

"I'm very good. Now."

"Are you free? I have some questions I need to ask you."

"Sure. Shall I come over?"

"How about we meet somewhere?"

"Okay. I'll pick you up. Be there in a minute."

The call ended. Tina's face expectant.

"She's coming over to pick me up."

"Yep. She has it bad. Wonder if she's always like this or if you are special?"

"I'm special, of course."

Tina smiled, lit a cigar, and poured tea. "Know anything about drones?"

"Not really. They are apparently popular and getting more so."

"Do you think they might help us?"

"Huh. Haven't thought about it. Off hand I'd say possibly."

"Thanks."

"Why?"

"I'm thinking of getting one. Want to stay on top of technology, you know."

"Ever since Johnson made you with that reversed image search, you've had a bee in your bonnet about technology."

She waved her hand. I suppose wishing I might disappear.

The doorbell rang. I went to see who it was. Bea was standing on the front step.

"It's Bea. See you later."

"Behave yourself, big brother."

I opened the door and greeted her. She'd driven over in the Maserati.

"Here," she said, handing me the keys. "You drive."

We walked to the car. I opened the passenger side door for her. She got in and I walked around and got in the driver's side. I adjusted my seat, the mirrors, and started the car. Beautiful sound.

"Where are we going, Harry?"

"Sebastian Joe's."

She giggled. "That's what? Six blocks from here?"

"Yep. But we're going to take the long way."

She squealed like a little girl. "I love you."

I looked at her. Yep, forty-seven going on twelve.

She leaned over and kissed me. "I love you, Harry. I do."

"Bea, we hardly know each other."

"It's okay if you don't love me. You do like me, don't you?"

"I like you very much."

"Good. I hope you fall in love with me one day."

I put the car in gear and drove around town for twenty minutes finding out what I could about the servants. Genevieve Stockman is the butler, forty-five. Been employed by Alicia for fifteen years. Genevieve manages the household. She lives in the house. Gets a 100K a year. Lottie Grosman is the chef, fifty-seven. Been the Harris household cook for ten years. Lottie also lives in the house. She gets 75K a year. Other staff are on call or hired when needed. Neither Genevieve, nor Lottie are married. Lottie, though, has a boyfriend who often assisted with meal preparation when Alicia had a big gathering. Bea has never seen Genevieve with anyone and suspects she might be asexual.

Information obtained, I drove to the ice cream shop. Bea once again insisted on paying. I had spumoni and she had Dreamsicle. With business out of the way, we talked about our pasts, future dreams, the weather, art, music, all the things people talk about when they like the person they're with. The ice cream was so good, I got green tea to go and Bea got a chocolate chip. Then it was back to West Franklin.

I parked the car in the driveway.

"I had fun, Harry. I haven't enjoyed a night out for a very long time." She kissed me and then was all over me. Her breath smelled of chocolate and her lips tasted of chocolate. "Make love to me, Harry, please."

"Bea, slow down."

Her chest was heaving. "I'm sorry. You must think I'm nuts."

"No, I don't. You're lonely. You need to get out of that house. Do something."

"You're right. I do." She took my hand and kissed it. "I wish we could be together."

"Not now. Be patient."

She took a deep breath. "Okay. I'll be patient. You do like me, right? I mean, I know I'm not pretty. I'm flat-chested. No shape."

"Bea. I do like you. Really. I very much enjoyed our time together. When this case is over, then we can get together. In the meantime, find a hobby."

"Okay. I will. Goodnight, Harry. I had fun tonight. You made me feel alive."

"Ditto, Bea." I got out of the car.

She got in the driver's seat. Rearranged the seat and mirrors, backed out of the driveway, and took off down the street.

I shook my head and entered the house. Tina was just coming out of the music room.

"Want my report now?" I asked.

"Sure."

We walked to the office, where I gave her my report. I left out the personal interaction. She didn't really need to know that. When I was finished she nodded and asked me to call David and Ed in the morning. Tina was pulling out all the stops. David gets a hundred and twenty-five bucks an hour and Ed gets seventy. Add that to Gwen's eighty and the city was spending a pretty penny to solve this case.

Then she added, "Oh, Harry, I bought two drones. They should be here by Friday."

"We don't know how to fly them."

"We don't. But Sam at Bloodhound does. He'll give us lessons. They'll add a new dimension to our surveillance capability."

"They don't have very long flight times."

"These do. Up to half an hour."

I raised my eyebrows.

"One other thing. Tomorrow I want you to see if you can find out if any of our suspects has hired a detective in the past year. Aside from Bea."

"Okay. Goodnight."

"Goodnight, Harry."

I went to my room and decided on a hot bath. While soaking in the tub I thought about Bea's words: "You made me feel alive." And my response: "Ditto." I'm fifty-three; was married and now divorced. Bea is forty-seven; was married, divorced, and is now a widow from her second marriage. Time flies and we rue the shortness of life. Yet isn't it our own fault we waste so much of what we are given? I made Bea feel alive tonight and she did the same for me. What more can a person do for another human being?

IV – Thursday, 6 March

I GOT BOTH DAVID and Ed at first go. While I had them on the line I asked if they or anyone they knew was working for our suspects, who I mentioned by name. They said, no.

After breakfast, I started making the rounds of the local agencies and all the freelancers I knew. One after the other said no, even when I brought President Grant into the discussion. Sometimes adding his twin.

For lunch I stopped at White Castle, was halfway through my dozen bacon double cheese sliders, when in walked Stinky Johnson. Why he's called 'Stinky', I don't know. I think his name is John or Tom. Anyway, he's meticulously clean, so maybe that's why. Once or twice a year he has the bad habit of going on a bender. He'll buy a case of almond or vanilla extract and get himself plastered. Go into detox, and then be okay for six to twelve months until he gets the next itch.

He came over to my table, we exchanged hellos, and then I gave him a Benjamin. "Lunch is on me, keep the change." He raised his eyebrows, shrugged his shoulders, and went to the counter. He was back in a few minutes.

"How've you been," I asked him.

"Well, Harry. Been busy since I last saw you. That case you guys got was grim, wasn't it?"

"It was." He was referring to our missing person case from last October which turned into one hell of a ride of terror through the geological underworld of Minneapolis. The same one in which Gwen lost her hair.

"Still no word on the trial date?"

"No."

The conversation meandered and we exchanged small talk on a host of subjects. I mentioned Alicia Harris. He put his burger down and a wistful look came over him.

"She paid well," he said.

"Really?"

"Yep. Simple surveillance and she paid me two hundred an hour. For a whole year. I blew it by going on a bender, lost the job. Made really good money on that job."

"When was this?"

"Most of last year and a bit of the previous year."

"Something simple like keeping an eye on the spouse?"

"Nah. Had me watching the head of Harris Industries. Kind of funny she wasn't the head, but the rich and famous..." He took a bite of burger.

I digested what he told me. Alicia was keeping an eye on Richards. I asked, "Do any digging on the head of Harris?"

"Nope. Just surveillance. I think she had someone else doing the digging."

"You ever fly drones?"

"Me? No. My cousin does, though. Gets some fantastic pictures."

"Really?"

"Yeah. I was thinking of getting one. Be a real asset on the job."

"Huh."

"You could fly the thing up to a window. Take pictures. No one would ever see you. If I'd had one I could have maybe found out what Richards and Alicia's woman butler were up to."

I took a bite of burger to keep my jaw from hitting the floor. Walford and Genevieve. Huh. Maybe the butler did do it. But what could Walford offer Genevieve to make her go against her employer. A fifteen year employee getting a hundred thousand a year, plus room and board. Probably gets benefits too. If she's working with Walford, something must've come between her and Alicia. Wonder if Bea knows? This was well worth the Benjamin.

Stinky was finished with his lunch. He thanked me and bid me farewell. I ate my last burger and drank water. Then got up and left, heading for home. This info ought to give us a more focused direction.

When I arrived at the little mansion on West Franklin, I found Tina in the office. The cigar smoke hung in the air. She was drinking madeira and looking through a file. I told her what I found out from Stinky.

"Very good, Harry. Call Gwen and tell her to focus on Genevieve. Ask her to dig into her background too."

I did so and then asked Tina what she was reading.

"The autopsy report. Seems whoever stabbed her knew a thing or two about killing. Didn't just stick the ice pick in. He or she maneuvered the handle to cut up and down and sideways and then a big circle. Did a lot of damage to Alicia's heart. She never had a chance. What's Bea's background?"

"Elementary education."

Tina nodded. After awhile, "I think we need to talk to Genevieve. I don't think the police have yet. If they have, Cal didn't tell me about it."

I called Swenson. He answered and I asked, "Cal, have you guys talked to Genevieve Stockman?"

"Hang on." He covered the phone but I heard him ask someone about the Stockman file. He came back on. "Yeah. Didn't get much. Why? The General wants to see it?"

"You got it."

"Okay. I'll be over later." He disconnected.

"Cal will stop by later."

Later proved to be during supper. We invited him to join us and he did. We were having pork chops, sauerkraut, potatoes, and a garden salad. I gave in to Tina's insistence we eat something that was breathing at one time, had blood, and brains. When finished, we retired to the office. I brought tea. Cal doesn't care much for tea, but he took a cup. Tina refuses to serve coffee. She thinks it's disgusting. I set out a plate of Russian tea cakes to make the tea more palatable for Cal.

He passed the file to Tina, who looked at it. "The usual," she said, "I want to talk to her."

"Okay. I'll set it up." He was going to say more, but changed his mind. "Thanks for supper. I'd best be going. I'll call when I got something set up with Stockman."

"Thanks, Cal," Tina said.

I saw Cal to the door, locked it when he left, and returned to the office.

"They don't seem to have a clue," I said.

"No, they don't. No surveillance cameras. No one admitting they were near the crime scene. No one sticking out as an obvious suspect. Apparently no one saw anything unusual." Suddenly Tina stopped. "Harry, didn't Cal say the family was pushing for resolution?"

"He did."

"What family?"

"Good question. Parents are dead. No siblings. Bea doesn't care."

Tina told her cell to call Cal. "Hey, Sweet Cheeks…"

I left to make a fresh pot of tea. When I returned, Tina had a fresh cigar going and a full glass of madeira at hand. I poured tea for myself, got out my pipe, filled it, and lit it. When I got it going and she still hadn't said anything, I asked, "What did Sweet Cheeks have to say?"

"The family lives out of state, except for one cousin. Martin Merton."

"Say it ain't so."

"It is."

"Martin Merton? And you think Beatrice is bad?"

She shrugged. "What can one say? Parents sometimes have no taste or thought of their child's future." She puffed on her cigar. "When Alicia went missing, Genevieve called Martin. He apparently called his father, who is the brother of the late Alicia's late mother. He's the one who's been raising hell."

"Where do they live?"

"The Harris side lives in Montana, Idaho, and Washington. The Merton side in Iowa."

"Do the family members own any stock?"

"Don't know. Told Cal we want to meet with Martin. He's a doctor in Rochester. Police haven't done anything with him because he's out of the metro area."

I looked over my notes. "I don't have a breakdown of who owns what. Ben Harris kept forty percent of the company and, with Walford's share, kept control. When Harris died, Walford formed a new alliance and cut out Alicia. She didn't care then. But something happened to change all that and we think it's the row with Bea's brother."

"I still don't understand the family's interest. Unless they know Bea doesn't want to keep the stock and are hoping she'll pass it on to them."

"Makes sense. But can they come up with six hundred million dollars."

"Your girlfriend is worth one hell of a lot of money."

"I know. Only she isn't my girlfriend."

"I'll ask her what she thinks."

"Don't bother."

"You remember last year when you asked me to find you someone more suitable than Tatty?"

"I do."

"I think Bea might be the one. She's obviously taken with you. I just might have to start cultivating this."

I shook my head. "Yeah, do that. Then for sure she'll be the killer."

Tina chuckled. "My, my, aren't we being positive."

I picked up my phone and dialed Bea's number.

She answered, "Harry." Her voice was all breathy. Maybe she was even salivating.

"Bea, I need some information."

"Okay."

"How much stock do Alicia's relations own?"

"Oh, I don't know that. Nobody tells me anything."

"Might Alicia have any reports?"

"She might. Should I look?"

"That'd be great."

"Only I don't know what to look for. Would you help me?"

"Bea..."

"I know, Harry, but honestly I don't know what to look for. Alicia never told me anything and Genevieve doesn't either."

"Okay if I come over now?"

"Sure. I'm not doing anything."

"I'll be there in a few minutes." I ended the call.

Tina had the biggest smirk on her face.

"What?" I said.

"She got you again."

"Business."

"Uh-huh. And just what kind of business you planning on taking care of?"

"Good grief."

I left the office, grabbed my hat and coat, and walked out to my car. I shook my head, hopefully to dispel Tina's innuendo regarding my going over to Bea's place. And Bea. All I could ask myself was, was she truly that ignorant? Maybe she was. I drove over to her place, parked on the street, walked up the walk, and rang the doorbell. A light came on, there was a shadow, and then the door opened.

"Hi, Harry!"

"Hi, Bea. Where's Genevieve?"

"She has the night off."

I walked in.

"Lottie's out, too. I'm home alone."

"Dangerous," I said.

"Harry, I didn't kill Alicia. I really didn't. You can investigate until the Big Bang un-Bangs itself. I didn't kill her."

"Bea, I want to believe you. I'm inclined to believe you. But I'm working and now you're working."

"Okay, Harry. Work before pleasure. Follow me."

She led me upstairs and into a rather large room. She turned on the light. Nothing spectacular about the room. It was done in shades of blue and green. There was a large desk and chair. Bookshelves on two of the walls. Paintings on the other two. Windows looked out towards the street. There was a sitting area with a couch, low table, and two chairs. A couple filing cabinets.

"The funeral is tomorrow. Memorial service, really. She's been cremated. I already have the box." Bea pulled open a drawer in the desk. "Here."

I looked. The box was plain. White. Rectangular. Curved top. There wasn't anything else in the drawer.

"What are you going to do with the ashes?"

"I don't know. She didn't leave any instructions."

I sat in the chair and began opening the other drawers. Three drawers on each side. One in the center. Paper, envelopes, stamps, stapler, scissors, letter opener, ink cartridges for the printer. Nothing spectacular. In the center drawer I found pens and pencils. She had a Mont Blanc fountain pen. A Princess Grace De Monaco, I believe. A thousand bucks. There was also a Parker 51 and an Eversharp Skyline. I held up the Skyline.

"Nice pen. I'm going to guess it was Alicia's father's?" I said.

"I think so, Harry. That and this one." She held up the Parker. "You want them? You can have them."

"No, Bea. They—"

She cut me off. "They're mine now, Harry. She gave everything to me. You can have them."

"The only one I'm really interested in is the Skyline. In my opinion, much better than the Parker."

"It's yours. My gift to you."

"Okay, Bea, thanks." I put the pen in my pocket. "Now for the filing cabinets."

The one contained personal stuff. The other held nothing but papers related to Harris Industries.

"We may have hit the jackpot," I said. But after two hours, all I found was that the voting shares of Walford Richards, Melody Johnson, Peter Dent, and Helmut Peterson constituted the majority. Walford held twenty percent and Melody, eighteen percent. Which meant Dent and Peterson held thirteen percent. Added to Alicia's forty percent, that left nine percent unaccounted for.

"Bea, do you recall any other large owners?"

She thought. "Walford, Melody, Peter, Helmut. Oh, yes, Lois Finch. Not sure how much she owns but it isn't much. Compared to everyone else, she has the smallest share."

"If Alicia and Melody got together, they'd have it all sewn up."

"Yes. That's what Alicia was hoping for."

"And if the family got Alicia's share, they still couldn't take control. They'd need others. Puzzling. Very puzzling."

Bea just looked at me.

"I assume Genevieve has an office?"

"She does. It's on the opposite end of the floor. She keeps the door locked."

"What's your relationship with Genevieve?"

"When Alicia was here, she didn't pay me much attention. But now, since I sign her check, she is more cordial."

"You're her boss. What are her duties?"

"She runs everything. She was Alicia's Administrator and I suppose now she's mine. But she's reluctant to share much with me."

"Bea, you are the boss or the principal in butler-speak. You need to let Genevieve know her place and your place. While you have all of this money, you need to know all about it. If she doesn't want you for a boss, then tell her to resign. And if she won't, fire her ass."

"What if she gets mad at me?"

"When you were a teacher, what did you do when a child didn't behave?"

"I talked to the boy or girl to find out what the problem was and then tried to solve it."

"And if that didn't work?"

"They went to the principal's office."

"Same here, Bea. Except going to the principal's office means you fire her."

I touched her cheek. "Bea, you have over a billion dollars. For all you know, Genevieve could be stealing you blind. You need some backbone here. Not everyone is going to like you. But if you like yourself, you can live with the dislike."

She was quiet. After awhile I thought maybe I'd offended her. Finally, she spoke. "Am I a likable person, Harry?"

"Yes, I think you are. All you need is confidence."

She giggled. "It's like in the Wizard of Oz and you're the Wizard bestowing on everyone what they want. Only they already have it. They just need to realize it."

I smiled. "Bright as a searchlight."

We were sitting on the floor. She leaned over and kissed me.

"Do you have the keys for Genevieve's office?"

"No."

"When is she coming back?"

"She didn't say. Tomorrow morning for sure. Probably tonight."

"I have to go to my car."

We walked down to the front door. I ran out to the car. I retrieved my lock picks and returned to the house.

"What are you going to do?" she asked.

"Try to pick the lock."

Bea led me to Genevieve's office. The lock was pretty simple. I went to work and the lock yielded. I opened the door and turned on the light. The room was small. There was a desk, filing cabinet, and a small safe.

The safe was locked. I looked for someplace she might have put the combination. I eventually found it on a sticky note stuck on the outside bottom of the center desk drawer towards the back. Nothing like having the combination to make opening a safe easy-peasy.

I rifled through the contents. Money. Correspondence. Jewelry. Handgun. I looked through the letters. Several from Walford. Most were from Dr. Martin Merton. I looked at several. They were love letters. The most recent was postmarked March first. I showed them to Bea.

"Wow. I had no idea. I don't think Alicia even knew."

"Yes. Very interesting, indeed." I put them back. "Let's go. We have enough information."

"Would you like tea, Harry?"

I started to say, no, and then changed my mind. "Sure. Let's have tea."

We went to the kitchen. I sat at a barstool while Bea did the honors. She looked so happy getting to do something domestic. I think she'd make someone a great wife. Maybe even me. When the tea was made, she set out a plate of cookies and poured us each a cup. Then she sat next to me.

Neither of us said anything. Our presence alone was a comfort to each other. No words were needed. Generally, I am a contented fellow but there are days and more often nights when I feel lonely. I looked at Bea and she looked at me. And I knew right then, I didn't have the willpower to say no. She knew it, too, for she took my hand and led me upstairs to her bedroom. Once there, I kissed her and fell head first down the rabbit hole with Bea at my side.

V – Friday, 7 March

I GOT UP VERY early. Bea came down with me to lock the door. I kissed her goodbye and promised I'd do my best to be at the memorial service. Driving home at three-thirty in the morning one sees the city at about its quietest.

"Well, Harry, you up and did it," I chided myself. "Fucking the suspects is not good protocol. You better pray she isn't the murderer." After a few minutes shaming myself, I said to my car, "You know, you wouldn't think it looking at her, but she is a wild thing. God, I can't remember ever having sex like that. She'd make the Pope give up celibacy."

At Tina's place, I parked the car, and let myself into the house. Of course, I had to reset the alarm. I went up to my room and crashed. My alarm rang. I shut it off. I woke with a start, looked at the clock, and swore. I flew through the shower, got dressed, and went straight to the office. Tina was there smoking a cigar.

"She good?" Tina asked without bothering to look up from her book.

"A gentleman never tells."

She smiled. "Grab something to eat. We're going to Bea's in half an hour to talk to Stockman. And, Harry?"

"Yes?"

"I should probably take you off the case."

"Tina."

She shrugged her shoulders.

I went to the kitchen, poured myself an orange juice, and grabbed an apple. I returned to the office and told Tina what I'd discovered. She sat back in her chair, chin resting on steepled fingers.

"Very good, Harry. This is a help."

▼

When we arrived at Bea's place, Cal was already parked in front. We walked up to the door, rang the doorbell, and Genevieve answered. She asked us to enter, took our coats, and then took us to a small sitting room on the main floor.

"What can I do for you?" she asked.

Cal said, "Just as a reminder, Justinia Wright is a consultant we've brought in to help us on the Alicia Harris case. She has a few questions for you."

"I already gave a statement to the police," Genevieve said.

"I read it," Tina replied.

Genevieve nodded. "What would you like to know?"

"You worked for Alicia Harris for the past fifteen years."

"That's correct. I was placed here one month after completing training with the late Ivor Spencer. I began working for Ms. Harris, July first, nineteen ninety-eight."

"What was it like working for Ms. Harris?"

"She was very hands-off. She wanted me to manage the household, as well as her financial and social affairs. Which I did. I gave her a report every month."

"What was your occupation prior to becoming a butler?"

"I was a nurse."

"How long were you a nurse?"

"Seven years."

"Why did you leave nursing?"

"Why does one leave any job? I didn't like it. I read about butlers and thought the job suited me. I quit my job and went to Ivor Spencer's school."

"Bea Pinneman is now your principal. How do you get along with her?"

"Well, enough."

"Would you elaborate?"

Genevieve hesitated. "Ms. Pinneman is not a knowledgeable or sophisticated person. She's very pleasant. She needs my services even more than Ms. Harris; however, her upbringing... She wants to do everything herself."

"She's gone on record saying she wants to give away all the money."

"Yes, I've heard her say that."

"Which means you'll be out of a job."

"Yes. Lottie, the cook, is already looking for other employment."

"How do you feel about that?"

"It's not for me to say, Ms. Wright. The money is not mine."

"Are you seeing someone, Ms. Stockman?"

"What do you mean?"

"Do you have a lover?"

"I don't see how that has any bearing on the case."

"It might if your lover was one of the suspects in the case."

"The butler profession does not preclude one from having a partner or spouse. However, life is much easier if one doesn't. Being on call twenty-four seven makes a personal life rather difficult."

Tina nodded. I knew she was debating whether or not she should discuss the information we had about her extra curricular activities. She went down a different road.

"Tell me, Ms. Stockman, what do you stand to gain from Ms. Harris's death?"

"Nothing. She left everything to Ms. Pinneman. In fact, I will probably have to look for a new employer. Which you have already pointed out."

"Thank you for your time, Ms. Stockman."

We left. Tina updated Cal regarding Stockman's meetings with Richards and Merton.

"Why didn't you say something?" Cal asked.

"I'm giving her rope," Tina replied. "I want to see what she does with it."

Cal nodded. He got in his car and drove off. We got in Tina's and headed back to her mini-mansion. Once home, Tina went to the office and I got ready for the memorial service. I told her where I was going and I'd be back soon.

She nodded and said, "A funeral is probably safe."

I just shook my head and left.

The memorial service was like any other memorial service. A minister spoke pious words. Friends and relatives said kind things.

Bea was discreet. We smiled at each other from across the room. I stayed in the back, observing. Martin Merton was present; as were cousins Paul, Bertie, and Rose. Uncle Robert and his wife, Elsie, made the trip. And Robert's sister, Margaret, also came to pay respects to her niece. Robert and Margaret are the late Elise Harris's brother and sister. I guessed there were about fifty or sixty others present. Some were friends and others were connected to Harris Industries, such as Walford Richards. Bea's brother was also present.

I found the music interesting. The adagio from Albinoni's D minor oboe concerto, Vaughan Williams' *The Lark Ascending* and his *The Solent*, Michael Manring's "Sung to Sleep," Debussey's *Claire de Lune*, Liz Story's version of Warlock's "Pavane," Skempton's *Lento*, and Ravel's *Pavane for a Dead Princess*.

The music was on a recording and cycled through twice before the eulogies began and then played after they were concluded. A rather eclectic array of tranquil, feel good works. I made a note to ask Bea about it sometime.

When the service was over, I slipped out, and drove home.

I hate funerals. They are, for the most part phony. The real person is not discussed. Only a sanitized version is talked about. Such lies and dishonesty are incongruous with sending the departed one on his or her journey to the other world. It demonstrates to me the extent to which we'll go to shore up belief in the make believe.

Near as I can tell there is no proof anything exists other than this life on this planet. Yet we discount what we have for something we don't have and which may not even exist! I'll get off my soapbox now. I just think delusion, especially self-delusion is counter productive. When I was homeless, I couldn't afford self-delusion. Not if I wanted to survive to see tomorrow.

I parked in front of Tina's place. My life here is good. I have few complaints. I lack for doggone little. I think about Bea. She is a billionaire and has no desire to keep the money. She'd probably be on top of the world loving and taking care of a man who loved her and cherished her. At base, how simple we are. And how complex we make things.

At that moment, I decided to give life with Bea a try. A friend long ago told me, "Harry, marry the woman who loves you." I was too young to understand his words at the time. Bea might not love me. Just infatuated. Or as the polys would say, New Relationship Energy. But if I didn't give us a try I'd never know.

▼

The afternoon passed slowly. Tina was at her desk smoking, drinking madeira, and reading. On a whim I went to the Get Rooked site and looked up Tat Trap. But noticed she hadn't visited the site for a couple months. I gave up the idea of challenging Tatty to a game of chess.

The arrival of the drones livened things up a bit. They were already assembled, but I had no idea how to fly them. I made a note to contact Bloodhound or Stinky to get the number of his cousin so I could learn enough to not wreck them on my first try. After cataloging them into our inventory and putting them away in the garage, I quit my desk and decided to cook.

The phone rang three times interrupting my preparations. Just David, Gwen, and Ed reporting in to Tina. I went on making pan-fried flounder; oven roasted potatoes, carrots, and rutabaga; sautéed broccoli with herbs; and a salad of spinach, arugula, lettuce, Persian cucumbers, and grape tomatoes. When everything was done, I let Tina know supper was ready. The phone rang. I saw the caller was Cal and Tina had picked up. In a minute she entered the dining room and announced, "We're going to Rochester tomorrow."

"Talk to the good doctor?"

She nodded.

"Thanks, Harry. Looks and smells delicious. I'm going to miss you, you know."

"Where am I going?"

"She hasn't asked you to move in with her?"

I rolled my eyes. "No."

Tina said no more. She just left the smirk on her face.

"Wasn't Merton available today?" I asked.

"No. He went back to Rochester right away after the services, apparently. We'll see him tomorrow after eleven."

"How are things going with David, Gwen, and Ed?"

"Good."

That one word answer meant she was cutting me out. I was on a need to know basis due to Bea. Tina wasn't taking me off the case. I was being relegated to second string. After supper, Tina went to the living room and I cleaned up the dishes and put away the leftovers. When done, I went upstairs to my room. I sat in my rocker and instead of reading the book I'd selected, promptly fell asleep.

VI - Saturday, 8 March

THE DRIVE TO ROCHESTER on US 52 is, for the most part, underwhelming. Flat farmland giving way slowly to urban sprawl. Rochester and the Twin Cities reaching out to embrace each other. Tina was driving as usual. I was in the passenger seat looking mostly out the window.

"I know you're pissed," she said. "What do you want me to do?"

I didn't say anything.

"Be that way. *You* fucked her. I didn't. And she's still a suspect and we're still working on the case."

Tina was right, of course. I only had myself to blame. Nevertheless, anger is irrational and I was angry.

"Harry, are you going to let a woman come between us? One you don't even know that well?"

Okay. That one hurt. Now she really had a point. "You're right. I crossed the line."

"I'm sorry, Harry. Really."

"I know."

There was a pause, then, "How was she?"

"You pervert! You're all nicey-nicey and you just want to know if I got a good lay or not. She-it."

She was howling with laughter. So I decided to have some fun of my own.

"Yes, she was good. And what's more, I am thinking of moving in with her."

We went from ninety to zero in less than ten seconds. We were on the side of the highway when the T-bird rolled to a stop. She twisted in her seat and stared at me.

"Are you serious?"

"Kinda."

"Oh, you little shit. No, you're older. You're a big shit. You're toying with me."

"Only kind of. I like Bea a lot, Tina. She's not an intellectual giant, but there's something incredibly sweet and sincere about her. She's a simple person. All I have to do is be kind to her, appreciate her, and she'll do anything for me. She's hungry for love. There's nothing complex or phony about her."

"Well, I'll be..." Tina put the car in drive and got back on the highway. "I guess I'll need to hire a new Man Friday. Maybe Genevieve."

I looked at her and we burst out laughing.

▼

In Rochester, we stopped at Newt's for lunch. I had a Shroom Burger and a Pearl Street Stout. Tina opted for a chicken sandwich and Starling Castle Riesling. Our bellies full, we headed over to Dr. Merton's house. Parked outside was Cal.

"I was beginning to wonder if you two got lost," he said.

"Lunch," Tina replied. "The place was busy."

"I take it you didn't go to Wendy's or Mac and Don's," he replied.

"Newt's," Tina said.

"No wonder. *You* have to go fancy."

"Swenson, do you even know what fancy is?"

I interrupted. "You two really need to get married. You got the routine down just right."

At the same time they said, "Shut up, Harry."

Now I got to smirk. We walked up to the house, rang the doorbell, and were let in by the tall, fifty-something man, identifying himself as Martin Merton. Of course, I'd seen him at the memorial service and had been briefly introduced. Cal introduced himself and we introduced ourselves. He didn't remember me. Introductions made, Cal explained Tina was a consultant and wished to question him regarding the death of his cousin.

Tina began, "Dr. Merton, how well did you know your cousin?"

"Moderately well. It's not as though we saw each other every day."

"Did you like your cousin?"

"She was nice enough. A touch arrogant. Not overly keen on family."

"How much stock does your family hold in Harris Industries, apart from what your cousin owned?"

"I believe we hold something in the neighborhood of less than a million shares. My father could tell you the exact amount."

"How many are you who own those shares?"

He thought a minute and then said, "Ten of us."

"The largest share of stock has now passed to someone outside of the family. What do you think about that?"

He shrugged. "What is there to think? It was bound to happen sooner or later."

"How often did you see your cousin?"

"Two, three times a year. Holidays."

"How did the staff treat you?"

"The staff? I suppose alright. Staff is staff."

"What about Bea Pinneman?"

"What about her? Nice enough. Don't know what Alicia saw in her. She's rather uninspiring. Something of a scared kitten."

In some ways that is true. Until you get to know her. Then she is actually quite fun. She's not, though, the life of the party type. And if she sticks out its not in the most positive way.

"Are you aware your cousin was trying to take back control of the company?"

"We'd heard. Would have been a disaster if she had."

"Why do you say that? You have no faith in her manager, Ms. Stockman?"

"If she let Genevieve run things, it might have worked out alright. The rumor was Melody Johnson was going to run things."

"What's bad about Ms. Johnson?"

"She's another insipid creature. Her late husband was okay, but Melody? One of those bimbo trophies for the Viagra set."

"At the upcoming stockholder's meeting, what is the family going to do?"

"I don't know there is much we can do. Walford will probably maintain control. Not a bad thing. He's served the stockholders very well."

"Why would someone want to kill your cousin?"

"I don't know."

"No idea whatsoever?"

"None. I live alone. All I can say is I was home, alone, when she went missing."

"Thank you, Dr. Merton."

Tina stood and shook hands with Merton. Cal and I did, as well. The good doctor showed us out. Standing by Cal's car, he wanted to know if Tina got anything. She replied, she did. He shrugged, got into the squad car, and drove off. We got into Tina's T-bird and headed for home.

"Did you really get something?" I asked.

"Oh, yes, Harry." But she wouldn't say more.

VII – Sunday, 9 March

Sunday. Generally speaking our day off. But working a case means no day off, except for me. I'm playing second string. David, Gwen, and Ed were hard at work. Tina was taking in info and processing it. I was tagging along with Tina or twiddling my thumbs. I made breakfast for us and afterwards took one of the drones outside to see if I could fly the thing without wrecking it. Nothing fancy. Just up in the air. Up and down the street. Hovering in the air. Then brought it in and looked at the pics. Pretty cool. Tina was impressed. Me, too. Maybe I don't need lessons after all.

Around noon, I walked to Bea's pile. Since Tina was cutting me out, I decided she could fix her own lunch. The wind had picked up and was pretty damn raw. Wind chills in Minnesota can be a killer. Today was nasty. By the time I covered the seventeen short blocks and one long, I was sure Bea would think the Iceman cometh.

I rang the doorbell. Genevieve answered.

"Hi Genevieve. Is Bea home?"

She nodded and let me in, told me to wait in the foyer, and disappeared into the nether regions of the house. In a few minutes, Bea appeared.

"Harry!" She squealed and darn near threw herself in my arms.

I hugged her and when I looked up I caught a fleeting glimpse of a disappearing Genevieve.

"Why are you here?" Bea asked.

"Had to get out of the house. Next thing I realize, I'm ringing your doorbell."

"No wonder you're like ice, walking all that way. Let's get you warmed up." She led me to the kitchen where I met Lottie. Nice woman. We exchanged a few pleasantries, then Bea asked if she had any soup.

"Yes, Ma'am. The beef vegetable from the other day."

"Good. Would you heat some for Harry and make tea, too?"

"Yes, Ma'am."

"We'll be in the living room."

"Yes, Ma'am."

Bea then pulled me along like a toy to the living room where a fire was burning in the fireplace.

"How cozy," I said.

Bea sat on the floor in front of the fire and I sat with her.

"I've decided to sell the house, Harry. It's too big."

"I'm not surprised."

"I was talking to Alicia's cousin, Martin. He said the family wants to buy the stock. They're willing to pay me one hundred fifty million up front for it and then ten million a year for forty-five years."

"What did you say?"

"No. I want to either give the stock away or sell it and give the money away."

"What did Martin say?"

"He didn't like my answer. He tried to convince me they were giving me a good deal. I told him I wasn't stupid. Why did I want to loan him money to buy my stock? What if they didn't pay?"

I smiled. No she wasn't stupid. A share in the hand is worth way more than a promissory note in the bush.

"I also decided to get a stockbroker…"

Genevieve entered with a tray and set it on the floor. "Anything else, Ma'am?"

"No. Thank you, Genevieve."

The butlerette left. I tasted a spoonful of soup. It was very good.

"Doesn't Genevieve have a stockbroker?"

"She does, but I don't trust her. Well, maybe that is unfair. I'd rather have one who is working for me. I have appointments with two tomorrow. Care to come along?"

"I just might. I'll see if I'm free."

"I'm glad you're here, Harry. I've missed you."

I took her hand in mine and gave it a squeeze. "I've missed you."

The fire, soup, and tea warmed me up. Bea didn't say much. She just had a contented smile on her face. When I was done, I asked her if I could look at Alicia's records again.

"Sure, Harry."

We went upstairs to Alicia's office. I found the file drawer of stockholder meeting minutes. Found the oldest and began looking through them. After a couple hours I'd pieced together a picture of Harris Industries' transition from Ben Harris to Walford Richards.

Harris sold off sixty percent of the stock to capitalize expansion. He was Chairman of the Board and CEO. His longtime friend, Walford, was COO. The purchasers of the stock were family and friends. The odd one was Lois Finch who, according to a note scribbled on one of the reports, was an old flame of Walford's. What was emphatic were the words, "Lois hates Wally".

When Harris died, the board chose Walford to succeed him. The choice was not unanimous. Quite a large minority wanted Bertie O. Harris, a son of Orville Harris, Benjamin Harris's oldest brother, to succeed Ben.

There was a big fight at the stockholder's meeting. The swing vote was Peter Dent. Alicia had scribbled in the margin after the vote Peter's son got a VP position to reward Peter for his support. And ever since then Walford has commanded the Richards, Johnson, Dent, and Peterson partnership to victory each stockholder's meeting.

The note of most interest was a simple circle of red ink around the name of Jim Johnson and his death date. Four years ago. Melody, the trophy wife, is now in command of millions of dollars. A nice prize for someone else looking to nab a trophy. How has Walford kept her in his camp? That is the question niggling my mind.

"Bea, can we ring for Genevieve?"

"Sure." She pushed a button on Alicia's desk.

Genevieve appeared. "Yes, Ma'am?"

"Harry wants to ask you some questions."

Genevieve looked at me. Her face blank.

"I've been looking through the Harris Industries stockholder's meeting minutes. Part of the investigation."

Genevieve nodded.

"Tell me about Melody Johnson."

She hesitated.

"Should I call Lieutenant Swenson?"

"No. Jim Johnson was a friend of Mr. Richards's father. He died four years ago of a heart attack. Two years prior, he had divorced his wife and married Melody."

"Did Mrs. Johnson get anything?"

"From what I understand, she got the house and the liquid assets. Mr. Johnson kept the stock. Mr. Richards apparently loaned him cash for operating expenses."

"The stock was used for collateral?"

"I don't know. That is a valid guess."

"So why does Melody continue to support Walford?"

"There's reason to believe he may be seeing Melody."

"Really. What reason?"

"Photographs of them together."

"Alicia had these?"

"No. I have them. Not here. In a safety deposit box. Wells Fargo."

"Who took them?"

"Alicia's cousin, Alex, took them with one of those drones. Alex is a son of Bertie O. Harris. He was here for a year looking for employment. The photos got him a job at Harris Industries."

"I can imagine."

"But Alex didn't like the work and quit."

"And that's why Walford's been seeing you. He's trying to get the pictures."

Genevieve is good. A testimony to her training. She didn't flinch at all. All she said was, "In his position, wouldn't you?"

I pulled out my cell and called Tina. "You may have kicked me to the curb, but listen to what I found." I told her of my discoveries. She thanked me and ended the call.

Genevieve asked, "Are we finished?"

"What did you hope to gain by hanging on to the photos?" I asked. "Let me guess. You were going to use them to get money, or try to, out of Walford in case Bea let you go."

Bea was shocked. "Oh, Genevieve! I wouldn't let you go empty handed."

Genevieve was impassive. "Thank you, Ma'am. That's good to know."

I said to Genevieve, "I'd get ready for a trip downtown. The police just might want to see those pictures."

"Yes, sir. Anything else, Ma'am?"

"No, Genevieve."

A half hour later Genevieve was on her way downtown for more questioning. Lottie, supper made, had gone out for the night. Once again, Bea and I were alone.

"You hungry, Harry?"

"Sure."

"Let's see what Lottie made."

▼

We ate vegetarian lasagna and salad. Afterwards we disposed of apple-raspberry cobbler and drank tea. We watched a movie. An oldie. *The Prime of Miss Jean Brodie*. When the movie was over, I turned to Bea. She searched my face, touched my cheek, ran her fingertips over my lips. I kissed my fingertip and touched her lips.

"Bea?"

"Yes, Harry?"

"The polyamorous community has a term for this."

"Term for what?"

"What we're feeling. It's called New Relationship Energy. It's the bridge from what might otherwise be a one night stand to a lasting relationship. At least it can be. You and I both know sometimes the bridge doesn't reach to the other side."

She nodded.

"We also know the intensity doesn't last forever, but even when the intensity has gone it doesn't mean the love is gone."

She nodded.

I took a deep breath. "I love you Bea Pinneman and I hope it lasts forever."

She covered her face with her hands and started crying. I took her into my arms and she wrapped her arms around me, burying her teary face into my shoulder. When she at last got control of her feelings, she lifted her head. "Are you sure, Harry Wright?"

"As sure as I can be. Right here, right now, I love you."

She stood up. "I don't know what to say. I mean, you really mean it?"

"Yes."

"Wow. I was so hoping, but I never thought... Then we made love and, well, it was beautiful and I hoped there'd be more, but my life doesn't work that way, and I, I don't know, I thought maybe that's all you wanted, I mean I hoped not, but..."

I stood and kissed her. Our arms went around each other and it wasn't fireworks or shooting stars, it was being on the beach at night with a full moon and the waves gently lapping at the sand.

We parted. "Will you stay the night with me, Harry?"

"I'll stay, Bea."

"I love you so much. From the moment you first smiled at me. I love you, Harry Wright."

We went upstairs. We made love together. Then we had raw sensual sex. Finally we kissed and caressed each other to sleep.

VIII - Monday, 10 March

I WAS IN THE office by nine a.m. Tina was already there. She looked up when I walked in. "Glad you're here. Thought you might be on your way to Jamaica."

I shook my head and sat at my desk.

She went on, "These drones take great photos. The ones Alex got of Walford are really sweet. Fucking Melody in his backyard. Couldn't be any better."

"How'd you get them?"

"Cal brought them over after he finished talking to Genevieve."

"I guess we got ourselves a new toy," I said.

"We? You're staying?"

"Of course I'm staying. I need a paycheck."

"Oh, that's right. Bea's giving away the money."

"Anything on the agenda for today?"

"Cal's bringing Mrs. Richards over this afternoon."

"You want me here?"

"I do, if you want a paycheck."

"Okay. This morning I'm going stockbroker shopping with Bea. When's Mrs. Richards going to be here?"

"Two-thirty."

"I'll be here. Bea should be by in a few minutes. I'm changing clothes."

"See you later."

▼

I was waiting when Bea pulled up in the Maserati. She gave me the keys and off we went stockbroker shopping. She liked the second fellow from Smith Barney. Arrangements were made to switch accounts and for the broker to begin selling off the stock. For lunch, we drove over to St. Paul, had fish and chips at Mac's, and then it was back to Minneapolis. There was a little time before Mrs. Richards was due to arrive. I invited Bea in. We stopped by the office.

"I'm back. Have company."

Tina looked up. "Good afternoon, Ms. Pinneman."

"Good afternoon, Miss Wright."

Tina then stood up and walked to the door. She bent down and hugged Bea. "Take good care of him. He's all I have."

Bea, tears in her eyes, nodded and said, "I will."

Tina went back to her desk and Bea and I went to the living room.

"Harry, what did Tina mean when she said you were all she had?"

"We have no living family. It's just she and I. We're it."

"I'm so sorry, Harry."

"No need to be. But since we got back into each other's lives, we aren't separating. We stick to each other like glue. Sometimes it's not the most happy union, but it is us against the world."

"No wonder she is so concerned. I'll take good care of you, Harry. She won't be sorry. And I won't take you away from her either."

"We'll get along fine, I think."

The conversation moved on and we talked until two-thirty when I went to the office. Passing by the door, the doorbell rang. I opened it and there was Cal and who I presumed was Mrs. Richards.

"Hi, Cal."

"Harry. This is Sarah Richards."

"Pleased to meet you, Mrs. Richards."

"Likewise," she said.

I took their coats and hung them up, then ushered them into the office. Tina stood. Cal made the introductions.

"Mind if I smoke?" Sarah Richards asked.

"Not at all," Tina replied.

Sarah put a filter-less cigarette into a holder and I got up to light it for her.

"Thank you," she murmured.

Tina lit a cigar. I opened a couple of windows slightly and turned on a fan.

Tina began, "Mrs. Richards—"

"Oh, call me Sarah."

"Very good. Sarah, your husband said he was with you the night Alicia Harris was murdered. Can you corroborate that?"

"Only up until I went to bed. I have trouble sleeping. I usually take something. When I do, burglars could pick me and haul me away and I wouldn't know it until I woke up." Sarah took a drag on her cigarette and exhaled a plume of smoke towards the ceiling.

"Did you take something that night?"

"Probably. I do more often than not."

"Do you and your husband sleep in the same bed?"

"Not usually."

Huh. There went Walford's alibi. Right out the window with the snoring.

"Are you and your husband happily married?"

"We've declared a cease fire. That answer your question?"

"It does."

"Walford knows how to make money. He's a mediocre lover, a lousy husband, and was a so-so father."

"You have children?"

"Had. Our son died in Vietnam and our daughter died from a drug overdose."

"I'm sorry to hear that," Tina said.

"I used to be like that Bea Pinneman. Mousey. Subservient. Afraid of my own shadow. Making one bad decision after another. But when one child dies, then the other, and you discover your husband's been screwing some other woman and that they're into bondage and spanking and all that shit, well, you either fall apart or get a backbone. I got a backbone. Walford and I had a come to Jesus meeting. I told him right up front he was not divorcing me for some bimbo like Melody Johnson. If he tried to do so, he wouldn't have a penny left to his name and he sure as hell wouldn't be with Harris Industries. I also made him put seventy-five percent of the assets in my name. Made him sign a contract. He has a pot to pee in and that's about it."

After hearing that story, I hoped Bea didn't turn into a ball-buster. But then I probably wouldn't give her reason to.

"Your husband has continued his extra-marital liaisons?"

"I don't have proof, but I don't need proof. I can tell when he has a fuck buddy and when he doesn't. If I were a betting woman, I'd put money down right now that he's fucking a tied up and spanked Melody Johnson. Maybe right at this moment while we're having this little discussion."

"Rumor had it that Alicia Harris and Melody Johnson—"

Sarah cut Tina off. "Yes, that was the rumor. And maybe they were. Although I can't see Melody being a carpet cleaner. But people do strange things for power and money." Sarah was quiet for a minute or so. Her cigarette had burned out and she put a new one in the holder. I started to get up, but she waived her hand indicating she'd light the cigarette herself. When she got it going, she said, "It's possible Melody isn't as stupid as I thought. Maybe she was playing Alicia and Walford against each other. Seeing who would come through with the better deal."

"What was the relationship between your husband and Alicia like?"

"Love-hate. Walford wanted in her pants in the worst way. He was crushed when he found out from Harris she was a lesbian. But he hated and despised her for her cavalier attitude towards the company. To Walford the company is everything. If he ever lost his position, he'd die. He lives for Harris Industries."

"Why wouldn't he fire Greg Pinneman?"

"Because Alicia wanted him to. Mostly that. Greg is a hot-head, but good at his job. He's a company man, too. Walford loves that. So, company man and to tweak Alicia is what saved Greg."

"Thank you, Sarah."

I raised my hand. "You have a question, Harry?"

"I do," I replied. "Sarah, you've had a lot of loss in life." She nodded.

"What is it that has kept you going?"

"First of all, Harry, I got a pair as they say nowadays. I had to make a decision. Either I was going to lie down and let Life walk all over me or I was going to take charge and Life was going to be my carpet. I chose the latter. I lost my children and I lost my husband. Those were my losses. But I have money and the things money can buy. I love roses and orchids, so I became a member of the Rose Society and the Orchid Society. I have many wonderful friends, both in the societies and outside. I have had my losses, but I've also had my gains. The most important gain being getting a pair."

"Thank you, Sarah."

"You're welcome, young man. Now Lieutenant, since Justinia is done with us, you can take me home."

Tina stood and I escorted Cal and Sarah to the door, gave them their coats, and they departed. I returned to the office. Tina's chin was resting on steepled fingers. She was mulling over what Sarah Richards had said. I collected Bea from the living room.

"I'm going to put you to work," I told her.

She smiled and her eyes gleamed with delight. We stood side by side in the kitchen. She's only five-three and weighs about a hundred pounds soaking wet. I'm five-ten and weigh in at one-ninety. We're an odd couple. But standing next to me, peeling carrots, I can tell she is very happy. And knowing I have helped her to feel happy gives me a good feeling.

When supper was ready I called Tina and she came to the dining room.

"I hope you like it, Miss Wright," Bea said.

"I think you can call me Tina."

Bea smiled. "You can call me Bea."

We didn't talk about the case during supper. Technically Bea is a suspect. But I think Tina has ruled her out. The conversation started out complaining about our endless winter. Then Tina got Bea talking about her future and what she'll do with her money. When we were done eating, Bea and I cleaned up.

"You have a good life here, Harry," Bea said. "I feel like I'm stealing you away."

"Bea, the only person I have in the world is Tina. She has Cal and other friends. Now I have you."

"I have Greg. That's it. Well, now you. I guess I find it difficult to believe I should have you in my life."

I told her what Sarah said. Bea laughed.

"That sounds like Sarah. Get a pair and put life under my feet. Okay, Harry Wright, when we're done here you are going to give me a good fucking. Do you hear me?"

I burst out laughing and she started giggling.

IX - Tuesday, 11 March

I DID AS BEA commanded last night. She slept in my bed and I admit the feeling of having a woman there was very good. Snuggled in my arms and falling asleep she muttered, "I prefer testosterone." All I can say is I'm glad. I briefed her on the morning routine. Tina doesn't say anything, or very little. I usually read the paper. But for today, Bea said she was going to serve us breakfast and she did. I shared the newspaper with her. With breakfast over, Bea and I cleaned up and she went home.

When I entered the office, Tina said, "She's a nice person, Harry."

"She is," I replied.

"I hope it works out for you."

"Me, too. Be nice having her around. Give me someone who can spell me on the cooking."

Tina chuckled. "Didn't know that was such an onerous chore."

"It isn't. But you might get more meat if she does the cooking."

"By all means, Harry, have her sub often."

"Thought you wouldn't object."

"Seriously, Harry, I hope this works out."

"Thanks, Sis. To change the subject, my money's on Walford. Do you think Sarah realized she was giving us the rope to hang him?"

"Probably." She paused, then said, "You know, Harry, blondes get a bad rap and we red heads get called all kinds of names. But one should never underestimate the trophy wife. The trophy wife uses her good looks and sex to get money, prestige, and power. Take Melody Johnson. She seduces Jim Johnson. He leaves his wife for her. But she ends up getting the short end of the stick, because there are no liquid assets. The money is tied up in the stock. When Johnson dies, Melody starts working on Walford. But finds out he too is hamstrung. Then along comes Alicia, who has everything to offer to a gold digger like Melody. The two were made for each other. The question before us is this: did Melody or Walford kill Alicia? Which one gained the most or lost the least with Alicia's death?"

"You're saying Bea's off the hook."

"I think so. At the time, she didn't have a pair. To quote Sarah. I don't think she could have done it. She doesn't have the connections to hire someone. Moreover, she's like most people: just wishing an act of God will come along and free them from their bad decisions. I think we need to focus on Walford or Melody. They're the key players in this drama."

"I still think Walford. He was afraid of losing Melody which meant loss of control."

"Valid. But Melody is a predator. She lives off of OPM."

"Other People's Money."

"Precisely."

"But why Alicia?"

"We don't know what Alicia told her. Perhaps... Well, we'll be best served by talking to Melody herself. Don't you think?"

"She's coming here?"

"This afternoon."

▼

Cal arrived fifteen minutes before our guest. "Here's the statement she gave us."

Tina took it and looked through it, then set it aside.

Cal said, "I have to say there's plenty of motive to kill Alicia Harris, but we haven't run across anyone with plausible opportunity, or even means. I mean how many people have ice picks around these days?" He was clearly frustrated.

"From the fact Alicia Harris is dead, someone did have the opportunity and the means. We just need to discover who." Tina started to light a cigar, thought better of it, and put it back in the humidor.

The doorbell rang and I went to the door. On the front step was a youngish woman, with short blond hair in a pixie cut. I opened the door.

"I'm Melody Johnson. I have an appointment to see Justinia Wright."

"Miss Wright is expecting you."

I invited her in and took her coat, hanging it on one of the coat pegs by the door. Looking at her, I could see why she was in the trophy wife business. With her on your arm, you might not need the little blue pill. I guided her to the office and to a place on the sofa. After I made introductions, I sat at my desk.

"You know, Miss Wright, I already gave a—"

"I know," Tina interrupted. "I read it. I'd like to ask a few questions."

"I don't see what more I can possibly add."

"I'll ask questions and then we'll find out."

"Whatever."

"Mrs. Johnson, do you own or have you recently owned an ice pick?"

Melody giggled. "I didn't even know what one was. I had to look it up."

I could see Tina mentally putting in the clutch and downshifting. "Mrs. Johnson, how long have you been Walford Harris's mistress?"

"Ever since Jimmy died. Wally had loaned Jimmy money. He said if I played with him, he'd forgive the debt. I had nothing to lose and maybe quite a bit to gain. Then Alicia came along and I saw Wally had been a real tight ass. I'm not into women, but I wasn't into S and M either." She shrugged.

"You're not with Walford Richards anymore?"

"You know, when I found out Alicia died, I said, 'Shit, there went something good.' But then I got thinking, you know I actually have money. It's just in all that stock. I think I'm worth at least a couple hundred million dollars. I'd never thought of the stock as money. It was just votes and I'd sign the proxy letter over to Wally. But that stock isn't just votes, it's money."

Tina nodded.

"I'm rich! All I have to do is sell it."

"Are you going to sell the stock, Mrs. Johnson?"

"I'm pretty sure I am. Maybe I'll go to Europe. Find a nice Frenchman or Italian. Or even a German. They're all business, those Germans, until they get in bed. At least that's what I've read."

"Does Walford Richards know?"

"No. Not yet. He's just going to shit when he finds out. His little empire. Poof! It's gone!"

Melody Johnson was very pleased with herself.

"You know," her voice was hushed and conspiratorial, "he likes spanking. Not for himself. He likes to spank women. Maybe men, too. I don't know. Anyway, when he finds out, it's like *he* will get a spanking." She giggled. Obviously she was very pleased with herself.

Tina stood. "Thank you, Mrs. Johnson. You've been very helpful."

"I have? You mean we're done?"

"We are."

"Okay."

I got up and walked her to the door, helped her with her coat, and opened the door for her. When I saw she was in her car, I closed the door, and returned to the office. Cal was getting ready to leave. He was shaking his head.

"Thanks for the entertainment," he said.

"Anytime." Tina's Cheshire cat grin lit up the room.

The rest of the afternoon and evening passed quietly. David, Gwen, and Ed reported by phone. Tina smoked cigars, drank madeira, and thought. I vacuumed and made supper. Bea called and said her broker had found a buyer for the stock. A German conglomerate. She was excited.

"Now all I have to do is give all the money away and I'll be free of Alicia."

I have to say, I'm happy for her. If only all of life's problems could be dispatched so simply.

At supper, I mentioned Bea had a buyer for the stock.

"Really? That was fast."

"Seems a German conglomerate was looking to buy a company doing what Harris does."

"Maybe Melody ought to know in case they want more."

"Good idea."

"Why don't you call her, Harry?"

"Melody?"

Tina nodded.

I called right then while it was fresh on my mind.

Melody Johnson's smile was obvious, even through the phone. I could feel it. She said, "I'm calling my broker right now. Thanks for the tip." It's a good feeling when you make someone happy.

After supper, I left Tina in the office, drove over to Bea's place, picked her up, and the two of us went to a movie. After the movie, she and I got a burger and then I spent the night at her place.

Tina was cooking up something. I just didn't know what. Then again, I'd find out soon enough.

X - Wednesday, 12 March

I WAS HOME BY seven-thirty in the morning and had breakfast ready when Tina showed up an hour later. She was her usual grumpy self. I let it pass. At quarter past nine, she went to the office. I cleaned up the kitchen and followed her. In rapid succession, David Nagasawa, Gwen Poisson, and Ed Hafner arrived to collect their pay. Just before lunch, Cal showed up. He wasn't overly happy. He stormed into the office.

"So, you had to go and be judge and executioner. Didn't you?"

"Good morning, Cal." Tina put a bookmark in her book.

"You couldn't let us do our job."

"Do you want to tell me what this is all about?"

"Ha. As if you didn't know. Sarah Richards called this morning to report her husband killed himself."

"Really?"

"Yeah, really."

"I put it at sixty-forty in favor of him doing so. Our will to live is quite strong, you know."

Cal sat and muttered, "Jesus H. Christ."

I've always wondered what the "H" stands for. Maybe it's just there because it flows well on the tongue.

"Alright, Miss Chief Judge and Executioner, let's have it."

"Didn't he confess?"

"There was a letter of confession."

"What more do you want?"

"The icing."

"I can't say I knew for sure Walford murdered Alicia, but there was no one else left. Unless a random killer who just happened to be carrying an ice pick happened along.

Last night I went to Walford's house. After eight, so Mrs. Richards would be asleep. He was there. Soaking up the Scotch. It seems, Melody had called and told him she was selling her stock to the same company Bea was selling hers to. Which meant the Germans had majority control."

"Wait a minute," Cal said, "the Germans?"

I explained, "Bea called me and said she had found a buyer for her stock and since Melody wanted to sell I gave her the name of the company so she could take it up with her broker."

Cal's face was red. "Setting him up." He shook his head.

Tina continued, "We talked for awhile and then I told him his world was gone. He was going to lose control of the company and I could track his movements to Wirth Lake on the night in question. He had motive and he had opportunity. Didn't matter if we didn't find the ice pick. A jury would most likely convict him. The circumstantial evidence was quite strong.

"He told me he'd been in love with Alicia since she was a little girl. Made him sick to find out she was a lesbian. Then, when she tried to steal his plaything, that was the icing. He'd been stewing and drinking all that day. He knew she'd be at the party. He decided to have a showdown with her. He wasn't going to kill her. Just threaten her. But they got to arguing and in a fit of rage he stuck the ice pick in her.

"I told him maybe he didn't want all of that in the news. Probably be bad for business. Apparently he agreed."

Cal was steaming. "I ought to—"

"Ought to what, Swenson? I had a talk with the guy. I didn't hold a gun to his head."

"This ain't the first time, Wright, you've gone off and played judge and executioner." He shook his head. "We have a legal system to determine if a person is guilty or innocent. "This isn't like the old West. We are beyond vigilante justice, beyond people taking the law into their own hands."

"I took nothing into my own hands, Swenson. I just had a talk with the guy and he made his own decisions."

"He ODed on his wife's sleeping pills."

"Well, I wasn't there to shove little pills down his throat. So, how am I judge and executioner? I repeat: I just talked to him and told him it was over. He could prolong it or not. The choice was his. Then I left and drove home."

Cal and Tina sat there staring at each other, not saying anything for forty-seven seconds. I timed it. Cal flinched first.

"Fine. I have his confession. The case is closed." He stood up and walked out of the office and out of the house. He left the front door open.

I got up to close it when a bright cherry red Maserati GranTurismo MC Stradale drove up and parked in front of the house. Out of the car bounded a skinny woman with shoulder-length brown hair. She ran up the sidewalk and threw herself into my arms.

"Harry! I just heard. Walford committed suicide and confessed to killing Alicia."

I kissed Bea Pinneman. "Yes. I heard, too."

"Oh, Harry! Now we can be together. I'm not a suspect anymore."

"No, you're not. Come on in."

She entered the house. "Oh, before I forget. Here." She gave me the car keys. "Now the car is yours. I'll bring the title over as soon as I get all that straightened out."

"What can I say? Thank you."

We walked into the office. Tina was smoking a cigar and drinking a glass of madeira. I walked over to Tina's desk poured a glass of wine for Bea and myself. I took two cigars out of the humidor and gave one to Bea. I held up my glass and said, "To victory and to us."

The Leaves Of Life
Fall One By One

1 – Wednesday, 18 September

Bea Pinneman gave away a billion dollars. I know because I was there offering her my advice on every dollar she passed from her hand to someone else's. She kept five million for herself to be used for school and living expenses while she got re-certified to teach elementary education. She gave ten million to her brother, along with Alicia's Jaguar. I finally accepted the cherry red Maserati GranTurismo MC Stradale, but turned down the five mil she wanted to give me. Knowing Bea as I do, I'm willing to wager the money is in a bank account somewhere with my name on it.

In August, the pile on 22nd Street sold. A non-profit paid something over 1.2 million for it. Bea sold all the furnishings and anything else connected to Alicia. She gave the cook and the butler two million each and sent them on their way to other employment. Bea found a nice house in Shoreview, on a lake; bought it, along with all new furnishings, and moved in on the 4th of September. She asked me to move in with her.

I was tempted, but I have my own demons and marriage is one of them. I guess I haven't gotten over my own matrimonial failure and I love Bea too much to get embroiled in something where I might lose her. Living together is too much like marriage in my book.

So I told her, "Beatrice May Pinneman, I love you, I just can't live with you yet. I'm afraid of a repeat of my marriage and I cherish you too much to ruin a good thing."

She kissed me and said she understood. I hope she was telling me the truth, because I really am crazy about her.

After she got settled into her new digs, I asked Bea what she did with Alicia's ashes. It didn't matter to me, but I was curious, given Bea's attitude towards her former spouse.

She said, "I did a very bad thing, Harry. I poured them in the sewer. Then I burned the box in the fireplace and threw those ashes in the sewer too. I've never hated anyone before, but I hated Alicia. Does that make me a bad person?"

"No, Bea," I said, "I don't think it makes you a bad person. We all exact vengeance in our own way. Pearl Buck tells in one of her books how the Chinese servant who was badly treated went up on the roof every morning and urinated so it would end up in the rain barrel which supplied water for the family who abused her."

Bea just nodded and I let the subject drop.

We haven't had any contact from Cal since the Harris case. He must be really pissed at Tina to let half a year and an entire summer pass without even so much as a text message. I asked her about him back in June. She shrugged her shoulders, blew out a cloud of cigar smoke, took a sip of madeira, and quoted Omar Khayyam:

Whether at Naishapur or Babylon,
Whether the cup with sweet or bitter run,

The Wine of Life keeps oozing drop by drop,
The Leaves of Life keep falling one by one.

In July, Tina, Bea, and I went to a bonsai show. Our friend and sometime freelancer, David Nagasawa, was showing. He won two blue ribbons. Tina isn't a plant person. She has her three cats. But at the show she met Norman T. Osgood. He not only likes plants, bonsai in particular, he's also a cat lover. Tina and Norm have been quite thick since meeting at the show.

I like Norm. He's far more chatty at breakfast than Tina. However, I'm still of the opinion Tina and Cal are meant for each other. I think they love each other and want to be together, but let too much baggage get in the way. Unfortunately they're just too pig-headed to see it.

Today dawned brightly. A beautiful September morn. Even Tina was chatty at breakfast. Bea and I texted silly nonsense back and forth. Tina once again asked if she needed to start looking for a new Man Friday. Once again I told her no.

After breakfast we retired to the office. Tina lit a cigar and started reading a book on her iPad. I sat at my desk, checked the bank balance, and realized we had no case and plenty of money. Two days ago we completed a high-profile kidnapping case. In the end it wasn't anything as dramatic as it had started out. A child kidnapped by his father because the mother wouldn't let him see the kid. Marital bliss and harmony continuing after the tie that binds is severed. Prior to the kidnapping case we had two rather routine surveillance jobs in which I got to use our new drones. I love drones for my work. I hate them when it comes to my privacy. Right after the Harris case, we were hired to conduct a little industrial counter-espionage. Something right up Tina's CIA alley.

Whenever we have plenty of money in the bank, Tina tends to get lazy and will even "retire" from detecting. She'll take up her paintbrush or schedule piano recitals or once in awhile go off to some remote place where cell phone signals have yet to go.

Suddenly all the glorious sunshine pouring into the office gave me a feeling of foreboding. At any moment I might have to run interference with her I-don't-want-to-be-a-detective mood. I know I sound all gloom and doom and on such a beautiful day I should have my feet up and enjoy it. But my paycheck depends on Tina working and since I like paychecks, I like her working.

The morning passed serenely enough. I busied myself dusting and vacuuming and made sure I had everything I needed for supper. Bea and Norm would be joining us. I made a light lunch of cream of celery soup and four different tea sandwiches: cucumber, roast beef and horseradish, camembert and fig, and sweet onion. When the table was set and the food on the table, I told Tina lunch was ready. We sat in the dining room and ate. She chatted away about nothing in particular and then started talking about Picasso's painting *Le pigeon aux petits pois*, which was stolen and is presumed destroyed. Uh-oh. She went on how she always thought it an intriguing work.

I was desperately searching for something to get her mind off paintings when the phone rang. Saved. I answered and the young sounding female voice on the other end asked to speak to Tina. I handed my cell to her.

The conversation on Tina's end went like this:

"Oh, hi, Trish."

"Uh-huh."

"Yeah, sure. I'm available. Foote's Piano Quintet, you said?"

"Uh-huh. Sure. Thanks for asking. Bye." She gave me my cell back and continued on about the Picasso. After a moment she saw I was looking at her. "What?" she said.

"Do you mind telling me with whom you just agreed to play Foote?"

"What makes you think I agreed to anything?"

"Because I know you."

"All work and no play makes Tina a dull girl."

"Uh-huh."

"What's your problem, Harry? Did I forget to give you a paycheck?"

"No."

"And there's money in the bank, right?"

"Yes."

"And you turned down five million dollars from Bea, right?"

"I did."

"So what are you bitching about?"

"You know."

"Huh." She got up and left the table.

A minute or two later she was playing Bantock's "Barcarolle in F minor" on the piano. I sighed. This might be the start of a very long fall.

I spent most of my afternoon working on supper. For starters I had mini mushroom pies, smoked salmon roses on rye toast, herring and beets on rye bread, and bacon and olive squares. A pot of Mexican grey squash soup was simmering on the stove and a stuffed capon was roasting in the oven. I was working on the fish course, a smoked haddock and rice kedgeree with Indian spice, when the doorbell rang.

The stove clock indicated the time was too early for Bea and Norm. I washed my hands. The doorbell rang again while I was drying them. "Impatient bugger," I muttered. With towel still wiping fingers, I walked to the door and opened it.

"Hi, Harry. Tina home?"

Our old friend, Cal Swenson, was standing before me. His face looked as though he had taken on the role of Atlas. Before I could answer, the strains of Liszt's piano transcription of Beethoven's Fifth Symphony thundered from the music room.

Cal said, "Yeah, she's home. May I see her?"

"Sure, Cal," I replied. "Come on in."

He entered the house and I guided him to the office. "We've missed you," I said. I noticed he was holding a plastic bag.

The look he gave me questioned my honesty.

"Truly," I replied.

He grunted in response.

I left him in the office and went to the music room. Tina was on the last dozen bars and I let her finish. When the last note played, I applauded, and announced, "You have a visitor. In the office."

"Who?"

"Sweet Cheeks."

A smile, every bit of which was worthy of Mona Lisa, appeared on her lips. "What does he want?"

"To see you."

"Uh-huh. You didn't call him, did you?"

"Nope. Scout's honor."

"Must be desperate." She got up and followed me to the office.

Cal was still standing when we got there. Tina went straight to her desk and sat, took out a cigar, and lit it. I sat at my desk.

"Well, Swenson," she said after a cloud of smoke was on its way to the ceiling, "what do you want?"

He walked to the desk and set the bag on it. "That's for you," he said and then took a seat.

"Are you Greek?"

"Huh? I'm Swedish and Norwegian," he replied. "You know that."

"Just making sure. Beware of Greeks bearing gifts, you know."

"Yeah, well, you have nothing to fear then."

"Guess not, Sweet Cheeks."

At the sound of his pet name, Cal relaxed a bit. Tina took out of the bag a box. She looked at it for a moment and then she smiled. A big warm genuine smile.

"Thanks, Cal."

"I had to search hell and beyond to find a box of those La Gloria Cubanas made in Miami."

"Thank you very much." She looked in the bag and took out another box. She opened it and the surprise on her face, well, I quickly snapped a picture with my cell phone.

"Where did you get this?" Her voice was soft and filled with awe.

"I had to search hell and beyond for that too."

I got up and went to her desk to see what the fuss was about. A bottle of 1952 Rutherford and Miles Malmsey. All I can say is Cal was really going out of his way to patch things up. And Tina was duly impressed. She got up, went to the couch where he was sitting, put her arms around him and kissed him. I thought one of them might suffocate, but at last she got up and returned to her desk.

"Glad you like my peace offerings," Cal said.

"I do, Cal. Thank you ever so much."

He looked at his hands. Cleared his throat, then managed, "Uh, Tina, I need—"

She interrupted with a simple, "Yes."

"Yes?"

"You want me to help you on a case and I just said I would."

"Oh, uh, yeah, I do. Uh, thanks. I really appreciate it."

I got up and left. I figured he didn't need me there listening to his *mea culpa*. I busied myself in the kitchen with supper. A half-hour later I heard the front door open and close. Tina entered the kitchen.

"What's the story?" I asked.

"Calvin loves me, this I know, for his gifts tell me so."

"You aren't telling me anything new. You two just need the license."

"It's more fun this way."

"Uh-huh. So what did you say yes to?" I opened the oven to check on the capon.

"He wants my help on a murder he's investigating."

"Right up your alley."

"Except I'm possibly on the list of suspects."

"Oh?" The kedgeree was ready, which left the beet and arugula salad.

"Seems someone got pissed off enough at Jared Copley to do him in. He was murdered a week ago. Cal suspects his wife and her boyfriend, but so far their alibi is holding up. They say they were at the house and no Copley. They left and came back. Found him on the floor very much dead. Next on the list are a couple former clients who've been sending him hate mail. And then there are Copley's paramours. Nothing like a jilted lover to pick up a knife and stick it into the one who screwed her."

"You got into a pretty big fight with him, didn't you? Copley, that is."

"You bet. The fucker wanted to stiff me on my Hopper pastiche, *Chow Mein*."

"Weren't there witnesses?"

"There were. I'm on the long list because I didn't threaten to kill him."

"Glad for that."

"Why thank you, big brother." She gave me a peck on the cheek. "I'll be in the office."

The beets and arugula were witnesses to my big smile. I finished the salad, made the dressing, and took the capon out of the oven to let it rest before carving. The doorbell rang. I went to the door and opened it. Bea threw herself into my arms, letting the screen door slam shut.

"Oh, Harry! I've missed you!"

"Your last text message was twenty-four minutes ago."

"You silly. I haven't *seen* you for *two* days." And with that she sealed her mouth to mine and sent her tongue exploring.

There was a knock on the door. Bea pulled away. Norm was looking at us. A big grin on his face.

"Hi, Bea. Harry. Mind if I come in?"

"Not at all, Norm," I said.

He opened the screen door and stepped inside. I hooked my thumb towards the office. He nodded and went in. I closed the front door. Bea set down her backpack and wrapped herself around me again. My arms went around her and I buried my face in her hair. She smelled faintly of spice, with woody notes.

"Mm. I love how you smell," I murmured into her hair.

"Oh, Harry, you make me so happy."

"Come on, Precious, help me finish up the supper preparation."

"Sure thing, Sugar Plum."

We walked to the kitchen, hand in hand.

Bea put the canapés on a tray and I poured glasses of Sercial madeira. We took the food and drinks to the living room and I went to the office to get Norm and Tina. Bea handed out wine as we entered the living room. Her glass, I noticed was empty. After she gave us our glasses, she poured herself another.

Norm snagged a bacon and olive square from the tray on the table and put it in his mouth. "How do you do it, Harry?" he said when it was gone. "Top drawer, man."

"Thanks, Norm. Basically, I follow the recipe."

Bea giggled. Tina drank wine. Norm took another canapé. "You have magic fingers," he said. Bea nodded vigorously and had a big smile on her face. Norm continued, "I follow a recipe and I end up with Frankenstein's monster."

"That's alright," Tina cooed, "you have other talents."

"Glad you think so, Sugar," he said.

"So was there anything else Cal had to say?" I asked

Bea, her glass once again empty, said, "He was here? Today? Wow. He hasn't visited in ages."

Tina shot me her What The Hell Is Wrong With You look. Norm said, "He's that cop you used to date, right?"

"Yes," Tina said. "He asked if I'd consult on a case and I said yes."

"Oh, so it's work," Norm said.

"Yes, it's work," Tina affirmed.

Bea giggled. "I *love* working on Harry." Realizing what she said, she giggled again and said, "I mean *with* Harry." She swayed gently in the breeze that wasn't there. Yep, two glasses of madeira and she's just about done for. Bea and alcohol don't mix well.

I put my arm around her. "Maybe we ought to eat," I said while guiding her to the dining room. She did okay with me holding her. Tina and Norm followed us. The three of them sat and I went to the kitchen to get the soup.

Norm and Tina were on one side of the table and Bea and I on the other.

"This soup is very good, Harry," Tina said.

"Harry's the best cook in the world," Bea said and started playing footsie with me.

"Thank you, one and all," I replied.

Prudy, Manley, and Isis jumped up on the sideboard and sat watching us.

"Did you feed them, Harry?" Tina asked.

"They have food."

"They're like the Three Stooges," Bea said.

Tina raised her eyebrows. These cats are her children. I chuckled. "And Isis is Curly." Isis is a hairless Sphinx.

Norm burst out laughing and Bea snorted her soup. Tina wasn't amused.

"Maybe we ought to talk about a safe subject," I said. "How about them Twins?"

Bea, overtaken with gales of laughter, almost slid out of her chair, which set the rest of us laughing. Yeah, Bea and alcohol aren't a good mix. There was more wine with the fish and capon. But we made it through dinner. Bea, though, was somewhere in the stratosphere.

After the meal, we retired to the living room. I served tea and biscotti. Tina, herself slightly loose, announced she'd be playing the piano part in Foote's Piano Quintet with a string quartet from Hamlin University. So that's what the earlier call was about. The one she didn't want to talk about.

"How about some music, Babe," Norm said.

"Sure, Peaches," she replied.

Peaches? She called him Peaches? Sheesh.

We moved to the Music Room. Tina has a Sohmer baby grand piano. A beautiful thing from the 1980's, made about ten years before Sohmer went belly up. Great sound. She sat at the keyboard. Bea and I sat on the love seat. She practically in my lap. Norm sat in a tub chair. Tina began with a Beethoven bagatelle and followed with a Chopin etude.

"How about something more modern?" Norm called out.

Tina played Joplin's "Kismet Rag" and then a medley of "Love is Blue," "So Happy Together," and "Walk Don't Run." When she finished, Bea weaved a path to Tina's side. She whispered to her and Tina burst out laughing. Bea, too, started laughing so hard she almost fell down. Thank goodness the piano was there for her to hold on to.

"Okay, Bea. Have at it," Tina said.

Tina started playing and Bea began snapping her fingers. Norm and I looked at each other. Normally, Bea's voice is soft and rather high pitched. So the smoky, sultry sound coming out of her mouth as she belted out the words to "Fever" had us all wide-eyed and open mouthed. Add to it Bea's seductive cavorting on and around the piano and, well, we had quite a show.

When the song was finished, Bea turned lust filled eyes on me and said, "Now, Harry. I'm on fire."

I got up, scooped her into my arms, and told Tina and Norm goodnight. Bea waved as we departed for my bedroom.

When we got to my room, she sighed, "Oh, Harry." Back to her soft, high voice, "I have it bad for you. I'm burning up with lust and drowning in love."

I kissed the little whisper of a woman in my arms. "I love you, Bea. Love, love, love you."

"I'm never going home, Harry, my darling. I'm staying here with you forever."

I kissed her again and lay her gently on my bed. She started unbuttoning her blouse but couldn't manage the buttons. I took her hands, kissed them, and set them by her side. I unbuttoned her blouse and when the last button was free, she was fast asleep. I smiled at her. This crazy, insecure woman makes me happy in a way no woman has for a very long time.

11 – Thursday, 19 September

MORNING CAME TOO EARLY and I had all the cleanup from the night before. An hour passed before I got the kitchen presentable to a degree where I could make breakfast. Toast, soft boiled eggs, and tea. Then, at the last minute, I decided hash browns and bacon might hit the spot too.

I was on my second cup of tea when Tina joined me in the dining room. I said the obligatory good morning and she grunted her usual acknowledgement. I poured her tea.

"Eggs? Bacon? Toast? Hash browns? I asked. Head shakes to one, two, and four. A nod to three. Toast it is.

I made her toast, buttered it, and gave it to her with a jar of orange marmalade.

"No Norm?" I asked.

"Left at two-thirty." The comment was meant for me, but she was staring at her iPad. After a moment she said, "Bea?"

"Sleeping."

Tina nodded, took a bite of toast, chewed, swallowed, and said, "Are you going to marry her?"

"Not today."

Tina nodded in acknowledgement. She was dressed in her usual navy blue skirt suit with a white blouse and emerald scarf. Her fiery red hair was done up in a bun on the top of her head.

I turned a page in the newspaper and ate a strip of bacon.

She shook her head in disgust at my handling of the newspaper while eating and said, "If you marry her you can live here, you know."

"Thanks for letting me know."

Tina nodded. She finished her toast and tea, announced she'd be in the office, and left.

I finished my breakfast and cleaned up the kitchen. Ran upstairs to check on Bea. She was still asleep. Back downstairs, I got a cup of tea, and made my way to the office. Tina was at her desk, looking at several sheets of paper, and smoking a cigar. A Muniemaker Long. Must be saving the La Glorias.

"We might as well start with Heidi and her boyfriend," she said.

Working. She was working. "When?" I asked.

"Whenever."

Huh. Not working too hard. "Want Cal here?"

"Sure."

"We have phone numbers?"

"Yes." She pushed a sheet of paper to the edge of her desk.

I got up and retrieved it. Back at my desk, I called Heidi, the grieving widow, at least in theory, and set up an appointment. I asked her to bring along Warren Asner, if she could, and she said she would. Next, I called Cal and he said he'd be at our place to watch Tina do her thing.

Before he hung up, he asked, "Did she really like the gifts?"

I told him she did.

"Good. See you later."

To Tina, I said, "Party's on for four."

Into the office staggered Bea, wearing one of my robes. She looked like a tsunami survivor. Tina took one look at her and a smile touched her lips.

"I don't feel too good," Bea managed to get out.

I got up from my desk. "Come on, O acolyte of Bacchus."

Tina snorted a laugh.

A faint smile appeared on Bea's lips. "Yeah, I'm a mess."

Arm around her, we walked to the kitchen. I sat her on a barstool and poured her a cup of tea. I got her a couple aspirin, too. "Want something to eat?" I asked.

"Toast."

I made her toast and set it before her.

"Thanks." She spoke so softly I could barely hear her.

I sat next to her and ran my fingertip down her cheek. She smiled. When she finished her tea and toast, she said she was going to go back to bed. I kissed her, picked her up, took her to bed, and tucked her in.

"Kiss me again before you go, my darling."

I kissed her, then went back down to the office. When I got settled at my desk, Tina asked, "Is she going to make it?"

"She'll be fine."

"Need to fatten her up so she can hold her liquor."

"Working on it."

"She's so skinny I'm surprised you don't lose her in the bed sheets."

"She holds on tight and says, 'Giddyap.'"

Tina laughed out loud, shook her head, and said, "Somehow with Bea that's not an impossible picture." She got up. "I'm going to tickle the ivories for awhile. What's for lunch?"

"Leftovers. HYWYR."

"Huh?"

"Help yourself when you're ready."

She frowned and muttered on her way out, loud enough for me to hear, "And he complains about me not working."

I stayed at my desk and cruised the internet seeing what I could find on our suspects. The result was not much, which is frequently the case when dealing with ordinary folk.

I walked out to the kitchen, filled a bowl with leftover soup, and nuked it. I filled another bowl with leftover salad. Then returned to the office with hot soup and salad. While I ate, I continued down the list of suspect's names Cal had provided to see if I could find anything on any of them. The one I found the most information on was Tina. Not that I was seriously entertaining her as a suspect. But what if Cal's gifts were his way of bidding her farewell?

A week ago. Sunday the eighth. I thought back to what we were doing then. Not good. I wasn't here. David Nagasawa and I were doing surveillance on the kidnapping case. Supposedly Tina was working, but I had no way to confirm her story. I got up and went to the music room where she was playing Debussy's "Reverie".

"Did you do it?" I asked.

"No."

"You're not just saying that, are you?"

"No."

"You'd swear to it on Mom's and Dad's graves?"

"Yes."

I stood there listening to her play. She stopped.

"What? You don't believe me?"

"I believe you."

"Like hell. Why are you standing there?"

"Listening to you play."

"Uh-huh. I'm hurt to think you'd even ask me this."

"I'm sorry."

"You really think I'd off him? He wasn't worth the time of day."

"At least if Cal asks I can say, no, and be utterly positive about it."

"Gee, thanks."

"I'm sorry."

"Just go. Shit. My own brother."

I left and checked on Bea. She was in the shower. A good sign. I went back downstairs and busied myself getting the office tidied up. Bea came in as I finished up.

"How are you feeling, Babe?" I asked.

"Much better." She came up to me and put her arms around me. "Harry, are you telling me the truth?"

"Probably, but about what in particular?"

"About not caring I was with a woman. Married to a woman."

"Honest, Bea, it doesn't bother me."

"Because I don't think it matters how one gets an orgasm. It's about if the person giving you the orgasm loves you. I mean a dick or a tongue can be just another kind of dildo. And that's what I've had all my life, just one dildo after another and I don't want to find out you were just a dildo too. You see?"

I nodded.

"Because I really, really love you, Harry, and I'd be crushed to find out you were just like the others. You make me feel good about myself. It's not a game, is it Harry? I'd die if it was a game."

"It's not a game, Bea. I wish I'd met you decades ago."

"Me, too. But we're together now. You and me."

"We're together, Bea, forever and ever."

She kissed me. I looked at her. Nothing special brown hair. No makeup. Boyish figure. Oversized t-shirt and cotton slacks in an attempt to hide her skinniness. No bra. Doesn't need one. Sometimes she wears an undershirt or a cami under her shirt or blouse. Yet when she smiles, someone flips on a switch and a thousand searchlights are beaming. Her eyes sparkle with mirth and merriment. At least since she's been with me. She's bright and witty.

I kissed her back. "I love you, my darling, and I'm yours. I'm not going away."

She sighed and held me.

Tina walked into the office and around us. "Feeling better, Bea?"

"I am, Tina. Thanks for asking. Do you have clients coming?"

"We do," I said.

"Okay. I'll make supper." She gave me one more peck on the lips and left.

"I like Bea," Tina said when she was gone. "She doesn't suspect me of murder."

"Good grief. I said I was sorry. Can't you forgive me?"

"Maybe. Oh, before I forget. Bea can live here."

"That was random."

"Not at all. She wants to be with you, Harry. To live with you. Even more, to be your wife. You aren't marrying her or moving in with her. I'm giving you the option of her living here."

"Thanks. And I'm sorry."

"Come here."

I walked to her desk. She kissed her fingertip and touched the tip of my nose. "I love you, too."

"Thanks and ditto."

The doorbell rang. I answered the door. Cal was standing outside. I let him in and he proceeded to make his way to the office. I followed him in.

"Bea's making supper," Tina said. "Want to join us?"

"Bea?" Cal asked.

"Bea Pinneman," Tina replied.

"The Pinneman woman married to Alicia Harris?" Cal asked.

Tina nodded.

"What's she doing here?"

"We're seeing each other," I said.

"Really? She bi?" he asked.

"She's a woman."

"Yeah, I know." He shook his head. "Working okay for you, Harry?"

"You bet. She's wonderful."

Cal looked at Tina.

She sang, "I'm just wild about Harry/And Harry's wild about me!"

Cal laughed out loud.

"Alright, you two," I said.

The doorbell rang. I went to the door and through the peephole saw the rest of the party and a gatecrasher. I opened the door.

"We're here to see Justinia Wright," the woman said.

"You're Heidi Copley?" I asked.

She nodded and said, "This is Warren Asner and this is our attorney, Harold Feingold."

I invited the group in, closed the door, and showed them into the office. I made introductions and made sure everyone had a seat. Feingold, I sat on the couch with Cal. Warren and Heidi each got their own chairs.

"Hopefully this won't take long," Tina said. "Mrs. Copley, how long were you married to your husband?"

"Uh, twen—, twenty years." Clearly the not so grieving widow was nervous. Very nice to look at. Can't imagine why Jared went after other women. Perhaps looks aren't everything.

"Did you love him?"

"At first. But then it just kind of withered away. He wasn't a nice person."

"I know. Why did you stay with him?"

"I don't know. I, I just did."

"Did you wish him dead?"

"Uh—"

"Don't answer that," Feingold said.

Tina smiled. "I already know the answer, Heidi. Of course you did. No abused spouse at some point in time doesn't wish the abuser dead."

Heidi's hands were clenched together and she was focused intently on them.

Tina continued, "The question remains, did you wish him dead enough to actually kill him?"

Heidi looked briefly at Tina and then returned to the examination of her clenched hands.

"Would you like a glass of wine?" Tina asked.

Heidi Copley's head popped up. The thirst was apparent in her eyes.

"No, she doesn't," Warren Asner said. For a man nearing seventy, he was in good shape. Not especially handsome, but careful about his dress and grooming.

"Mr. Asner, how did you meet Mrs. Copley?" Tina asked.

"She was one of my students many years ago."

"I mean recently."

"I was in town to discuss a show with Jared Copley. Heidi was in the gallery and I recognized her. Found out she was Copley's wife and she'd given up painting. Damn bastard kept telling her she was no good until she believed him. Not true, of course. Heidi has plenty of talent. Just needs a gentle hand to bring it out."

"And you're that hand," Tina said.

"I am. I'm proud to say, I am. So many wasted years. But I got Heidi painting again. When she has enough paintings, we're going to hold her own exhibition. Solo. She's excellent. She'll be famous one day."

Tina nodded, then pointed to a painting on one of the office walls. "What do you think of that painting, Mr. Asner?"

He looked at it, then got up and took a closer look. He turned around and said, "Looks like a John Francis Murphy. American Tonalism. Is it?"

"No. It's a copy I made of his *Afternoon Light*."

Asner looked again at the painting, then resumed his seat. "You're very good, Miss Wright." I gave him points for paying attention to my introduction. He continued, "Heidi is every bit as good. It's a shame Copley didn't see it."

Heidi's face brightened at the praise. From what I could see, she's a lot like Bea.

"When did you arrive in town, Mr. Asner?"

"I gave all this to the police."

"Humor me."

"No."

Tina raised her eyebrows. She stood and said, "Very well. Thank you for your time."

"That's it?" Feingold said.

"If your clients aren't going to cooperate, yes, we're finished," Tina said. "I will get my information, though. Rest assured."

Swenson was smiling. Cal always likes it when Tina gets pissed off and she's working with him. He can sit back and watch the bloodhound go to work.

Feingold hesitated, then stood. Asner and Mrs. Copley followed suit. I got up to show them out.

In the foyer, I said to Asner, "You made a tactical error back there. If you're guilty, it was a strategic blunder." To Feingold, I said, "Good luck."

I handed a business card to Heidi Copley. "In case something comes to mind."

I returned to the office. "They're gone," I said. "I gave Heidi a business card, told Asner he screwed up, and wished Feingold good luck."

"Jackass," Tina said. "If they're available, I want all three. Stinky, too, if he's on the wagon."

Cal let out a laugh. "You're pissed. This ought to be good."

"Come on, Sweet Cheeks. Drink?" Tina walked over to the couch.

"Sure. Why not?" Cal replied. "Beer?"

Tina wrinkled her nose.

"Yeah. We have beer, Cal. What would you like? Leinie?"

"Good man, Harry."

"Original? Creamy Dark? Red Lager? Hoppin' Helles?"

"Damn. You have the whole brewery here?"

"Nope. Half."

"I see that. I'll take Original.

Tina and Cal went to the living room. I went to the fridge, got the Leinenkugel for Cal, and from the cupboard got a wine glass for Tina. After serving boss and guest, I went back to the kitchen to help Bea but she had everything under control. Even had the table set. I added a plate and tableware for Cal.

"We have company. Cal Swenson," I told Bea.

"Oh. Okay," she replied. "We should have enough."

"What did you make?"

"Just a hamburger stew with dumplings and a salad."

"Sounds good to me. Want a drink?"

"I think I'll pass, Harry."

I kissed her forehead. "Mind if I serve wine with your stew?"

"No. Ten minutes we can eat."

"I'll let them know."

I told Tina and Cal ten minutes to chow time, then uncorked a couple bottles of Alexis Bailly Country Red. Stew and dumplings done, I carried the pot to the table. Family-style tonight. Bea brought in the salad and a dressing she made. I called Tina and Cal.

The four of us sat at the table. I poured wine for Tina and I. Bea passed and Cal asked for another beer, which I retrieved from the fridge.

Tina ate a spoonful of stew. "This is good, Bea."

"Thanks," Bea replied.

"Harry," my sis continued, "I'd like them all here no later than nine tomorrow morning, if you can arrange it. Your job is to get every piece of data you can find on the internet about Asner. If you run across something we need to track down in person, let me know."

"Okay, Boss."

"After Asner, see what you can find on everyone else."

Cal smirked. "I see the General hasn't lost her touch."

"Nope," I replied.

Tina then focused on Bea. "How long are you going to be staying with us?"

"I, I don't understand," Bea stammered.

"Talk it over with Harry. You can move in if you want."

Cal's eyebrows shot up his forehead.

Bea said, "Really? Wow! Thank you, Tina. Oh my God. This is like Christmas."

Tina smiled. "Glad I could make your day. What are you doing tomorrow?"

"I have class."

Tina was thoughtful. "Can you skip it?"

"I really shouldn't. Why?"

"We're going to be very busy the next few days. I need someone to man the store. Just in case."

"Oh. Well, uh, I suppose I can help. I'll email my professors."

"Great. Thanks, Bea. Harry will tell you what to do."

Business taken care of, the conversation shifted to other topics and we had a pleasant meal. Cal and Bea seemed to hit it off. And that's a good thing with Bea moving in and Cal back in the picture. At least I hope he sticks around. After supper, Cal took off, I made phone calls to David, Gwen, Ed, and Stinky, and Bea and I drove out to her place to pack up clothes and other belongings she might want to have with her. She was moving in. I gave her two rooms to use. One for a bedroom and the other to use for a living area in case she wanted private time. We'll have to move the bed out and move a couch and table in.

I know one thing. Bea needs a new wardrobe. She gave away all the clothes Alicia wanted her to wear and Bea's sense of fashion? Well, it would be fine for shoveling pig shit. I think I'll ask Solstice, Tina's renter, to go shopping with Bea. I find it rather fascinating that my darling is forty-seven and in so many ways she's fifteen.

She didn't want to sleep alone and with the two of us now living together why should she? Her breathing is soft and she is curled next to me fast asleep. I don't mind Tina pushing Bea and I together. If left to me, I'd probably never make the move. And I love her too much to lose her.

III – Friday, 20 September

THEY WERE ALL IN the office by nine. Tina, Bea, and I ate breakfast early and were waiting. I introduced Bea to the gang and told them she was our pinch-hitter Gal Friday. When we were all together, Tina gave us the scoop she'd gotten from Cal.

"Good morning and thanks for coming on such short notice," she began. "You may or may not know that Jared Copley, owner of Copley Gallery, was murdered a little over a week ago."

"I saw that," David Nagasawa said.

"You had some art work with him, didn't you?" Gwen Poisson asked.

"I did," Tina replied. "The list of suspects isn't long, but long enough. Cal Swenson wants to finger the wife and her boyfriend but so far hasn't been able to break their alibi. Our job is to break the alibi or finger one of the other suspects."

"Who else is involved?" Ed Hafner asked.

"Two artists, Randy Hedgeman and B. A. Palmer, were sending hate mail to Copley for turning off potential buyers."

"Why would Copley do that?" David asked.

"Hedgeman's work is very similar to that of Libby Hanson. Hedgeman claims Copley was sabotaging him in order to promote Hanson. Palmer claims Copley dumped her because she wouldn't go to bed with him."

Gwen nodded her agreement with Tina and added, "Hanson and Hedgeman were an item for awhile then broke up. Copley represented both but liked Hanson's work better. Rumor has it Copley screwed her a couple times and that's why she and Hedgeman broke up."

"Thanks, Gwen," Tina said. "Didn't know that bit. Next on the list is Ron Wimbly. His wife, Linda, had work in Copley's gallery. Cal verified she and Copley were having an affair. Wimbly is a hunter and has guns. He threatened to blow Copley away if he ever touched Linda again. Pete Nyquist is just behind Wimbly. Nyquist's girlfriend supposedly let Copley dip his wick in exchange for letting her display in the gallery for free. Nyquist said he was going to break Copley's neck."

"Anything odd we should know about?" David asked.

"Supposedly a burglar broke in and killed Copley. Police didn't find any unexplained fingerprints. The knife used to kill Copley had no prints at all. If the burglar was wearing gloves, why would he wipe the knife?"

David nodded.

"Your assignments are as follows: David, I want you to go to Chicago and find out everything you can on Warren Asner. He's Heidi Copley's boyfriend. You're licensed in Illinois, right?"

"I am."

She pushed a folder to the edge of her desk. "That's what we have on him as of right now."

David got up and took the folder. He took a quick glance at the contents and returned to his seat.

"Gwen, I want you to find out what you can about Heidi." Tina pushed another folder to the edge of her desk.

Gwen got up and took the folder. She returned to her seat and looked through it.

"Ed, you get to find out what the cuckolded husband and lover have been up to." She held up two folders for him to take, which he did.

Tina looked at Stinky. "You have perhaps the most important job, Stinky, so don't let me down."

"I won't, Miss Wright."

"Good. I want you to interview all the neighbors. I'm looking for someone who may be able to contradict Heidi's or Warren's alibis. Okay?"

He nodded.

She held out a folder to him. "Pictures of Heidi and Warren and info about both of them."

Stinky got up, retrieved the folder, and returned to his seat.

"Cal and I will go over the crime scene and the gallery. Harry will be available for backup if you need it and doing computer searches. Bea will answer phone calls."

Gwen asked, "Heidi is with Asner at his hotel?"

"That's the last info we have," Tina replied. "She hasn't been back to the house. Any other questions?"

No one said anything. Tina continued, "Harry will give you expense money. Thanks, again."

I doled out the cash and one by one they departed. When they were gone, Tina grabbed a jacket and said she would be back sometime in the afternoon. She left by the back door.

Bea asked me, "What do I do?"

"Answer the phone when it rings. I'll set it to roll over to your cell."

"Okay."

"I'll be here, unless someone needs my assistance."

"Okay."

"Feel free to do whatever you want. Just make sure you answer the phone."

She came close to me and kissed me. "Are you okay with me living here?" she asked.

I kissed her back. "I'm very okay with you living here."

She kissed me again. "I have one regret, Harry."

I kissed her again. "You do?"

"Mm-hm. I'm too old to have your baby."

"Yeah. Not much we can do about that."

"You still love me? Even though I can't have your baby?"

"I love you, Bea. Baby or no. You bring joy to my life."

"I'm so happy with you, Harry, my love."

"I, too, have one regret."

Her face became serious. A child who thinks she's done something wrong. "What?" She breathed in her quiet voice.

"I have to work instead of making love to you for the remainder of the morning."

A smile stretched from ear to ear. "God. I'm so horny."

"Later, my temptress. I have to work."

She kissed me. "I'll get supper prepared and then hit the books."

"Good plan, Babe."

Bea left and I got to work searching the internet for little tidbits of data on our suspects, starting with Asner. By half-past noon my eyes were bleary; my mind, mush; and my stomach was growling. I found my sweetheart in the library studying.

"Hey, can you take a break for a bite of lunch?" I asked.

"Sure. May I make you something?"

"Nope. I'm going to treat you to White Castle."

"Are you serious?"

"You bet."

"Harry, I love White Castle. Oh, my God. We are meant to be together. It's destiny."

"There you have it. Come on, Babe. Those sliders are calling our names."

"I'll drive!" she squealed.

Bea drove us over to Lake Street and into the parking lot of the White Castle. We ordered our sliders, fries, and onion chips and when the order was ready took it out to her car to eat. We ate, talked about the present and the future and made love to each other with our eyes. The past we left alone. Painful and gone, why go there? We have right now and we have the rest of our lives. The time has come for us to maximize our joy. When the food was gone, she drove us home. I made tea when we got there. She took a mug to the library and I, to the office.

Tina showed up a little before supper. She went to her desk, poured herself a glass of madeira, and lit a cigar.

"Find anything?" I asked.

"Not much."

"Me neither. Nyquist was arrested for a domestic three years ago. That's the only excitement."

"What's for supper?" Tina asked.

"Don't know. Bea made it."

"Huh. Is she taking over chef duties?"

"I was busy all day."

"So you were."

Bea poked her head into the office and said supper was ready. Tina made her way to the dining room. I swung by the kitchen to see if Bea needed help. She said no, and I continued on to the dining room.

"Did you leave off the two artists intentionally?" I asked Tina.

Bea brought in a plate of zucchini stuffed with rice, mushrooms, and beans. She returned to the kitchen.

"No," Tina responded. "We'll check on them. At first glance, they were just venting their frustrations. Cal didn't uncover any past history of violence."

"Okay."

Bea returned with a bowl of mashed potatoes and gravy. She also set out bottles of Alexis Bailly Country White and Country Red. I poured wine for us and Bea dished up zucchini.

"Was Copley's house truly broken into?" I asked.

"Looks that way. If a set up, whoever did it got it right."

"These are really good, Bea," I said.

"Yes, they are," Tina concurred.

"Thanks. Just trying to earn my keep."

"You're Harry's S.O.," Tina said. "You're family now."

Bea hid her face in her hands and started crying. Tina looked at me. I shrugged. After maybe half a minute passed, Bea lifted her tear stained face and said, "You are so kind and gentle and wonderful. Both of you. I've not had anyone treat me like this for a very long time."

Tina smiled. "Ask Harry how gentle I am. Anyway, you don't have anything to prove. Just so you know."

Bea nodded. Tears running down her cheeks, which she wiped with a napkin. I reached over and took her hand and gave it a squeeze. She smiled.

We ate our way through the food and drank enough wine to make our hearts glad. We talked about nothing in particular. Bea announced she'll rent out the house in Shoreview once she has everything moved out. After supper, I made tea and Bea served the apple pie she made.

Dessert finished, Tina went to the living room and Bea and I cleaned up. She and I then joined Tina.

"Tomorrow, Harry, I'd like you to take a look at our hate mailers," Tina said.

"Will do."

To Bea she said, "Tomorrow you and Solstice are going shopping."

"Who's Solstice?" Bea asked.

"My renter," Tina replied. "An artist who's rich daddy pays her rent for the apartment converted from the former servant's quarters next door."

"Oh. What are we shopping for?"

"Clothes," Tina said.

Seems Sis and I are on the same wavelength.

"Clothes? I have clothes."

"You're Harry's S.O. He might have no taste, except for what's in his mouth, but I do. If you look good, he'll look good."

"Oh." Then Bea got a big smile on her face. "Okay. I've never been good at picking out clothes. But I do want Harry to look good. So I'll do it and hopefully Solstice will teach me how to do it on my own."

Tina smiled and lit a cigar. I decided this called for a pipe and some port. I got a pipe and tobacco and a bottle of Warre's Warrior Porto. I poured wine for everyone, then raised my glass and said, "One for all and all for one."

IV - Saturday, 21 September

SOLSTICE SONATA PARKER KNOCKED on the backdoor at five to ten this morning. She's tall with a boyish figure, like Bea. Unlike Bea, she knows makeup and clothes and is knock down dead gorgeous. She wears her blond hair long and curled. Tina once said she was every man's wet dream. She was wearing a dress with belted waist, somewhat full skirt, and defined shoulders. A faux hourglass shape. Bea was wearing slacks and a shirt.

I made introductions, kissed Bea goodbye, and she and Solstice went off arm in arm. Solstice has a Land Rover, but Bea insisted on driving. I'm interested in finding out how they get along. Solstice has a confident expectation people will defer to her. I think it comes with growing up rich. Bea grew up working class and has an underlying deference. Yet she can be very assertive when she wants something. Like wanting me for instance. I'll be watching to see if they return arm in arm.

Tina was in the office sifting through data and I was staring at the computer screen when the phone rang. Caller ID notified me the caller was Ed. I told him to come in and entertain us with his findings. He said he was on his way.

"Ed have anything for us?" Tina asked.

"Wimbly is apparently clean and Nyquist's skipped town from the looks of things."

"You didn't find anything on Nyquist other than the domestic, did you?"

"No."

"Monday, pay a visit to the courthouse. See what else, if anything, you can find."

"Will do."

"See if Cal can get his people to track him down."

"Okay. If not, we do a skip trace?"

She wrinkled her nose. "I suppose."

The phone rang. I answered. "Hi, Harry. Gwen. I'm on my way. I think Heidi's story checks out. But Tina can read my report."

"See you in a bit, Gwen." I ended the call and said to Tina, "More bad news. Gwen thinks Heidi's story is solid."

Tina frowned. "Still leaves Asner and if Heidi knew about it she's an accessory."

"If she knew about it."

"Not likely she'd be in the dark."

I shrugged and went back to the computer. But the doorbell rang. I got up and went to the door, opened it, and let Gwen come in.

"Hey, Harry."

"Hi, Gwen. Go on in."

I closed the door and followed her into the office. She said, hello, and took a seat.

"So you think Heidi's story checks out."

"I do, Tina." Gwen got up and gave Tina her report, then returned to her seat.

"She had motive," Tina said.

"Yes and no."

"No?"

"Well, why would she kill her husband when Sir Gala-had was rescuing her?"

Tina shrugged.

"I just don't see her doing it," Gwen said. "It's all in my report."

"Thanks, Gwen. I'm just disappointed."

"Yeah. Well, somebody did it. Anything else?"

"Not now."

"Okay. I gotta buzz. Catch you later." Gwen got up and headed for the door. I followed her, showed her out, and showed Ed in.

We greeted and he went on into the office. He said "hello" to Tina and she reciprocated.

"What do you have for me, Ed?"

"Linda Wimbly has been having an on again, off again affair with Copley for five years. Three months ago they were on and Ron Wimbly found out. That's when he threatened to blow Copley's head off. But Linda and Copley were seen together as recently as two weeks ago. Wimbly was having his wife followed by Northstar Investigations."

"Interesting."

"Pete Nyquist seems to have left town. Rather suddenly, too. Four days ago. He, like Wimbly, seems to like the type of woman who found Copley attractive and was willing to cheat on her man to get what Copley had to offer. Three years ago Nyquist was with Bonnie Johnson. Bonnie got involved with Copley, Nyquist found out and smacked her around pretty good. Nyquist got arrested for domestic but Bonnie refused to press charges. He then threatened Copley saying he'd break his neck if he touched Bonnie again and a couple months later Nyquist dumps her. Then a year ago he's dating Malinda Gordon and she lets Copley screw her in exchange for him not charging her any commission for selling her art work. Pete finds out and again threatens Copley. Malinda, though, left Nyquist. Don't know if she continued seeing Copley or not. Maybe Nyquist decided to get outta Dodge thinking the cops might think he acted on his threats to Copley."

Tina nodded. "Maybe. Anything else?"

"No. Here's my report." Ed handed Tina several sheets of paper.

"Thanks, Ed."

Ed voiced his appreciation for the work and left. I made sure the door was closed. I swung by the kitchen. There was still tea in the pot. I poured a mug and returned to the office.

My call to Cal concerning Nyquist was still unmade. I made it and he answered. I passed on the info about Pete Nyquist and recommended he put a man or two on to track him down. He said he already had a boss and didn't need two, but thanked me for the info. He ended the call.

We hadn't heard from David Nagasawa or Stinky Johnson. David I could understand, being he was in Chicago. But Stinky, I didn't know. Maybe he hadn't been able to talk to everyone.

The phone rang. The caller ID told me the caller was Cal.

"Hey, Cal, found Nyquist already?"

"Yeah, right. You should get a show on Comedy Central. Hey, tell the Red Baron I'm sorry but I'm passing the skip trace back to you. Can't spare anyone to run one."

"Will do."

He rang off. To Tina I said, "Sweet Cheeks sends his love and regrets he can't do a skip trace on Nyquist."

Tina put on her perturbed face. "See if Gwen or Ed can do it."

"Righto."

I called Ed. Yeah, he was available, he said. And he'd get right on it.

The sun was in the west. Suppertime would be soon upon us and Bea and Solstice were still not back.

"I'm going for a drive over to Art Song's for wings," I said.

"Don't be skimpy. Get plenty," Tina replied.

I looked at the Maserati but got into my Ford and took off for the Midway in St. Paul. On the way there I turned over what we had, which wasn't much.

Unlucky Pete Nyquist had been made a cuckold twice by Copley via his unfaithful girlfriends. But Copley didn't die due to a broken neck, Nyquist's favorite threat. Linda Wimbly couldn't stay away from Copley, but Copley had not had his head blown off as Ron Wimbly had promised. Then again maybe one of them had become a convert to sharp instruments.

Heidi, thus far, was still squeaky clean, despite the suspicions of Cal and Tina. We still had Asner, Hedgeman, and Palmer to check out. But what if one of Copley's paramours had stuck the knife in him? Maybe Bonnie or Malinda. Perhaps Libby, upset because Copley was screwing her twice over? Or maybe the perp was a real burglar and everyone's barking up the wrong tree. Or maybe we're dealing with a lover we haven't tracked down yet.

Thank goodness Art Song's arrived in view before I had half the planet on the suspect list. I went in, ordered a couple bushels of wings to go, along with sides, paid, waited, got the grub, and, back in the car, turned around and drove home.

When I got back, Bea and Solstice were home, having beaten me by five minutes. I gave Bea a kiss and asked Solstice if she wanted to eat with us.

"Sure, Harry. Tina said you were getting Art Song."

Bea's face was questioning what all the fuss was about.

Solstice, in her Georgia twang, said, "Girl, they are the bomb. They're rock star. Once you've had Art Song's wings, you'll gladly die and give up heaven to have just one."

"Okay," was Bea's reply.

"You just wait, Bebe. You just wait."

Bebe? Solstice calls Bea, Bebe? Huh.

The three of us put the food on the table. While doing so I asked how the shopping went.

"Rock star," Solstice said.

"I have some very nice outfits, Harry," Bea said.

"Some? Count 'em. Fifteen. Plus shoes. Hope you didn't max out your credit card."

Bea smiled. "I'm okay."

Solstice shrugged. "If you say so. Are we eating? I'm, like, starving." She snatched a wing and began devouring it.

"Go ahead," I said. "I'll get Tina."

I went to the office. Tina was smoking a cigar and staring at papers on her desk.

"Grubs here," I said.

She sighed, got up, and followed me to the dining room. We ate, drank wine, talked mostly about the shopping spree, although Solstice and Tina got off on a tangent discussing post-punk retro-futuristic stream-lined modernism. Or something like that. After supper, Bea modeled her clothes and I have to say she looked downright sexy and desirable. Tina was very impressed, commenting Bea would now be turning heads and I'd better make sure I had a tight hold on her.

Fashion show over, Solstice told Bea to come over to her place tomorrow for makeup tips. She said goodnight and left. Tina lit a cigar and returned to the office. Bea and I sat before the fire in the living room.

"Tina seems preoccupied," Bea commented.

"Yeah. It's bugging her. She hasn't found the thread to pull to unravel the fabric. This case should be simple. Yet it's proving to be quite elusive."

"You like the clothes, Harry?"

"I do, Bea. You look stunning in them."

"Do you think I'm pretty."

She was fishing. Every man, no matter the truth, thinks his woman is beautiful. And I'm no exception. I decided to be honest. "No, Bea, I don't."

That wasn't what she was looking for and her face showed it. She turned her face away from me, stood, and started to walk away.

"Bea."

She stopped.

"I don't think you're pretty, because you're beautiful."

She turned around. "Thanks, Harry, but I'm not really. I'm Bea the flea. Who am I trying to kid?"

I jumped up and closed the distance between us, gently took hold of her shoulders, and looked her in the eyes. "Bea Pinneman, you are the most beautiful woman in the world. I'm proud to be seen with you and proud to call you my girl."

"Thanks, Harry. The words are nice, but—"

"I'm serious, Bea. You're the Venus de Milo."

"Now I know you're teasing me."

"I'm not."

She searched my face. "I'm beautiful to you?"

I nodded.

"Really?"

"Yes. You're not pretty, you're beautiful."

She put her arms around me and laid her head on my shoulder and started crying.

"What's the matter?" I asked.

"I don't deserve this. I don't deserve you, Harry Wright."

"Obviously you do, Bea Pinneman, because we met and we're together. Forever."

She looked at me. "I'm not—"

"You are, Bea. You're beautiful. Start telling yourself, 'I'm beautiful', 'I deserve happiness'. Tell yourself every morning and every night."

In a barely audible whisper she said, "I will."

"Good. Because my lover isn't junk."

She giggled. "God. I'm so lucky. Finally. After all these years." She took me by the hand and began pulling me towards the stairs. "Come on. I bought a couple of things that are for your eyes only."

After seeing what Bea had to show me, all I can say is, "Tiger, tiger, burning bright in my bedroom this very night."

V – Sunday, 22 September

I WOKE AND FOUND myself in an empty bed. Bea's room was empty. "Probably downstairs," I muttered to myself. I showered, shaved, dressed, and descended the stairs. Sure enough, Bea was downstairs and I found her in the kitchen. She was dressed in skinny leg jeans and was wearing a white blouse with ruffles, fitted at the waist and flaring over the butt and abdomen. She wore a simple necklace of gold and emerald green stones.

"Wow! What a knockout," I said.

Bea blushed. "You really think so?"

"You bet." I took her in my arms. "God, you smell good."

"I bought a new scent to wear in the day time. It's called Aqua Universalis. I take it you like it."

"You smell like you just came out of the shower."

"Good. That's what I wanted."

"You making breakfast?"

"I got water on for tea. I was thinking eggs, sausage, and toast."

"Sounds good."

"Want to help me?"

"Babe, anything to be near you."

"God, Harry, I'm the luckiest girl in the world. Why do you love me? I mean, I wanted you so badly and I actually got you."

"I love you because you are so lovable. Yeah, you threw yourself at me and it was a bit off putting. But I realized we both wanted the same thing: a sweet, kind, and gentle person who loved us and accepted us, warts and all. So I said, Does it matter if she's a crazy nympho?"

"Harry!"

"And my answer was, no. Because I really truly liked and understood the crazy nympho who wanted someone to love her for who she was."

"Oh, God, Harry." She hugged me. "You're going to make me cry again."

"Not now. We have breakfast to make."

"Am I really a nympho?"

"Damn close."

"Don't you like sex?"

"Well, yes, I do. I also like to sleep."

"We sleep."

"Yeah, I guess we do at that." I gave her a kiss and whispered, "Don't change."

"Don't worry."

We worked together and breakfast was ready by nine. Tina arrived in the dining room shortly after. We were already seated. She grunted a hello to us and poured herself a cup of tea. After a couple of sips, she stabbed a sausage with her fork and conveyed it to her plate. Per our routine, Tina read her iPad and I the newspaper. With Bea now in residence, the new routine was I shared the paper with her. By nine-thirty Bea and I were finished eating and just drinking tea. Tina poured a second cup and speared a second sausage.

Halfway through the sausage, she said, "Find Stinky. I want to know what's taking so long."

"Will do."

She finished off her sausage, downed her tea, and left the dining room. Within a few minutes, the sound of Arthur Foote's Suite Number One for piano came from the music room.

"Not a good sign," I said.

"What do you mean?" Bea asked.

"It means, my sugar plum, she's frustrated. And Tina being frustrated is not a good thing. Want to come with me and see if we can find Stinky?"

"Sure. I'll drive."

We cleaned up the kitchen and I explained about Stinky's habit of going on a bender occasionally.

Bea's only comment was, "Really? Vanilla extract?"

"Or almond," I added.

She shivered.

The kitchen presentable, I called Stinky's number but no answer. We got into Bea's car and off we went to north Minneapolis.

Being Sunday morning, downtown was quiet. Drizzle started falling when we crossed the light rail tracks. Stinky lives up in the Cleveland neighborhood on 35th, off Penn. His house is a little two-story expansion. I think he inherited it from his parents. Bea turned down 35th and I instructed her to stop in front of the house. His old 1992 Buick Roadmaster sedan was parked in the driveway. The beige monster made Bea's Fiat look like a toy car.

She and I got out of her mini-car and walked up the walk to his front door. I rang the doorbell and we waited. I rang again and we waited some more. Nothing. I tried the door. It was locked. We went around to the side door. It too was locked.

"Doesn't look like he's home," Bea said.

"That or he's passed out."

"Oh."

We went back to the Fiat and got in. I entered a number in my cell. "Hey, Jim, Harry Wright here."

"How's things?"

"Fine. Say, Stinky Johnson isn't on a job for you, is he?"

"No. I called him and he said he was working for Tina."

"Yeah, well, he hasn't reported in and I'm trying to track him down."

"If I see or hear from him, I'll let you know."

"Thanks, Jim. Catch you later."

I ended the call and thought about what to do next.

"Maybe something happened to him," Bea said.

"Possible."

"Should we call the police?"

"Not yet. We're going to check Detox first."

"Oh."

Bea started the car.

"Eighteen hundred Chicago," I said.

She put the car in gear, turned around using the driveway, and headed back the way we came. We arrived at Detox and inquired, but he wasn't there and hadn't been. We checked Hennepin County Medical Center, but he wasn't there either. I told Bea to take us home. When we arrived at Tina's pile, Bea parked and I let us in the back door. Piano music greeted our ears. Given the rather incomplete nature of the sound, I figured she must be practicing her part of the Foote Quintet.

I sighed and poked my head into the music room and told her Stinky was missing in action. A very unladylike word came out of Tina's mouth. I went to the kitchen to make tea.

Bea announced she was going to Solstice's for her makeup lesson.

I replied, "Okay, Babe. See you later."

The tea kettle filled with water and heating, I selected tea and waited for the water to boil. While waiting, I wondered what could possibly have happened to Stinky. Despite his annual or semi-annual bad habit, he was pretty doggone reliable. So this was unusual. Although he had gone off on a bender in the middle of an investigation before. Was this another one of those unfortunate times? I hoped not. But rather that than something bad.

The tea kettle whistled. I poured water to hot the pot, rinsed, and poured it into a second pot. I put tea leaves into the first pot and poured in the boiled water. The timer I set for four minutes.

Tina came into the kitchen. "You making lunch?"

"Tea. We have leftovers."

She nodded. "You're getting lazy. Maybe I shouldn't have invited Bea to stay."

"Good grief."

"Don't worry. I won't fire you. Might dock your pay, though."

"Double good grief."

She chuckled and began pulling food out of the fridge. When the counter was piled high with containers, she spooned coleslaw on a plate and put four wings next to the slaw.

"I'll be in the office. Join me when you're done here." She left.

The timer rang. I stirred the leaves in pot number one, emptied the water out of pot two, decanted pot one into pot two, and finally poured myself a cup. I too put wings and slaw on a plate. I decided to add a couple of dill pickles to the pile and took it all into the office.

Tina had poured herself a glass of Sercial madeira, drunk half of it, then plowed into the wings and slaw. I drank tea and started in on a wing.

"Was it burglary?" I asked.

"No. I don't think so. Looked good at first, though. Whoever broke in wanted Copley."

"The reason?"

"Number one, nothing of importance was stolen. A few pieces of jewelry and a small sculpture from what Heidi told the police. The place was trashed to make it look like burglary, but even that wasn't consistent with a professional. Number two, Asner and Heidi claim the lights didn't work when they arrived the second time. The circuit breaker had been flipped."

"Huh. Shades of 'Play Misty for Me'."

"Yeah. If true. It's possible they made up number two." She rustled through papers on her desk, found the one she was looking for, skimmed it, shrugged, and said, "Asner's prints were found on the box. Could have been a plant."

"So who's the most likely candidate for knife wielder of the year?"

"That's the question. Isn't it?" Tina took out a pad of paper. "Okay. Let's start. Heidi Copley." She wrote on the pad of paper. "Wife. One time artist. Motive?"

"Sure. Plenty."

"She had motive. Plenty of opportunity. The weapon was at hand. Her own butcher knife. Means? The knife, of course. Does she have the strength to drive home a knife in such a manner that would kill Copley?"

"I'd say maybe. If angry enough."

Tina wrote on the pad and tore off the sheet. "Warren Asner." She wrote on the new sheet.

"He had plenty of motive and certainly has the strength," I said. "He looked very fit when he was here."

"He did, indeed." She spoke while writing, "Motive. Plenty. Opportunity. Yes. Given his arrival time in town. Means? He could pull it off."

"I think, though, it makes the most sense for those two to be working together."

"I suppose. Aside from ridding the world of a bastard, Heidi will gain the insurance money. Two hundred thousand according to Cal."

"Not a lot, but more than you'd get with a poke in the eye from a sharp stick."

Tina looked at me and shook her head. "Asner is an art professor and an artist in his own right. Not top tier, but decent." She tore off a sheet of paper and wrote, saying the name "Randy Hedgeman."

"We haven't talked to him."

"No, but the police got a statement. Despite the hate mail, motive is weak. Another gallery picked up his work and he's doing well. I've met Hedgeman. He's not gay, but somewhat effeminate. Maybe metro-sexual is a better description. Rather tall and lanky. Can't see him sticking a knife into someone. Might ruin his manicure."

"Okay, Hedgeman, a long shot. What about B. A. Palmer?"

"Betty Ann is another long shot, I think. Again, despite the hate mail. According to her statement to the police, she was out of town."

"What was Hedgeman's alibi?"

"He was taking photographs of the city skyline for possible future work and ate his supper at Burger King."

"Not something someone is likely to corroborate."

"No." Tina wrote on paper. "But sounds entirely possible."

"What about Palmer? Is her alibi good?"

"She went up north, alone. Police confirmed she checked into the motel for which she had a reservation.

Duluth. Doesn't mean she couldn't drive back to the city and do the deed."

I nodded. "No, it doesn't. Why was she in Duluth?"

"Looking for inspiration."

"What about Ron Wimbly?"

"Plenty of motive. Cal noted he's something of a hot head. But Ed talked to Wimbly's buddies and they were all playing poker the night of the murder. Unless they're all in cahoots, I think we can rule him out."

"Sounds like it. Unless they're covering for him."

"Unless." Tina tore off a sheet of paper. "Now Linda Wimbly is another story. She admitted she and Copley were going to take advantage of the poker game and meet at a motel. Linda said she showed up, but Copley didn't. She tried calling but no answer."

I interrupted. "Her call show up on his phone?"

"His phones were taken."

"Convenient."

"For the perp. When he didn't answer, she went home."

"Maybe instead of waiting, she stuck a knife in him."

"Possible."

"Where was the motel?"

Tina looked on a sheet of paper. "Near Cannon Falls."

"Advance registration?"

"No."

"So she has no alibi."

"Not really."

"Could she have done it?"

"Physically? Probably. I don't see a motive. Copley was promoting her work and it was selling."

I frowned. "Lover's quarrel? They were on again, off again."

"Possible. Seems weak to me."

"That brings us to Pete Nyquist," I said.

"Ed's working the skip trace. Nyquist's disappearance doesn't put him in a favorable light. Let's set him aside until Ed locates him."

"Okay. Bonnie Johnson. One time girlfriend of Nyquist."

Tina started writing on a new sheet of paper.

"She's not an artist," I said.

"No, she isn't. She's the only one who isn't an artist or associated with an artist."

"That's interesting."

"It is. According to her statement, she met Copley in the bar where she was working. Bartender. One night he asked her out and she accepted."

"She know he was married?"

"Apparently."

"Why'd she go out with Copley?"

"Copley looked like he had more money than Nyquist."

"Huh. Screws Copley in the hopes of some payola. She could have settled on the fee up front."

"We don't know what gifts he gave her."

"Cops didn't ask?"

Tina looked at some paper. "Apparently not directly."

"Motive?"

"Nothing clearly established."

"Maybe he started giving her gifts from Walmart instead of Nieman Marcus."

Tina looked at me, shook her head, and said, "Maybe. Let's talk to her tomorrow."

I wrote a note to call Bonnie Johnson.

Tina started writing on a fresh sheet of paper. "Malinda Gordon. Another long shot. No ongoing relationship with Copley. Got her free display and, when the time was up, got her paintings back. Motive, probably none."

"Which leaves Libby Hanson, Hedgeman's rival."

"Let's talk to her, too. The police don't have much on her. Tomorrow, if we can."

I added Libby to the list.

Bea poked her head into the office. "I'm back."

"Get in here," I said. She entered and all I could manage was, "Wow!"

Solstice had curled Bea's hair and dolled her up with some rouge, bright red lipstick, mauve eye shadow, black eyeliner, and mascara.

Tina nodded. "You look stunning, Bea."

"Thanks, Tina." Bea's face was bright red, as though she'd forgotten to leave the tanning booth.

"I'm going to have to start carrying a club," I said.

"Harry!"

"God, Bea. The guys are going to be horning in on my territory."

"I'm so embarrassed."

"Don't be, Bea," Tina said. "You look beautiful. Solstice highlighted what nature should have and didn't."

Bea smiled. "She did a good job. I didn't recognize myself."

"We're going to eat out," I said.

"We are?" Bea said.

"Yep. Murray's. You joining us, Tina?"

"You want me along?"

"Yes. Come with us, Tina," Bea said.

"Okay."

"Great." I looked up Murray's website and booked a reservation. "Got it for eight."

Tina stood up. "I think we're done for now. I'm going to play the piano."

She left and Bea sat on my desk.

"You're beautiful, Babe."

"It's just makeup, Harry."

"It enhances what's there. Put makeup on a frog and you have a painted frog."

Bea smiled. "I love you, Harry. You're so good to me."

"I love you, Bea. My ex rather soured me on love. You've changed that."

"I'm glad."

"You hungry?"

"I am. I didn't have lunch."

"Let's get some."

"Some?"

"Food, you nympho."

Bea laughed. "God, you make me horny."

"I don't want to smudge your makeup."

"I hate this stuff already."

I stood up. We put our arms around each other and eventually made it to the kitchen.

VI - Monday, 23 September

FIRST THING IN THE morning, I called Stinky. No answer. Next, I called Cal and told him Tina wanted to talk to Bonnie Johnson and Libby Hanson. He said he'd see what he could arrange. Bea was making breakfast. I went over what I'd dug up in deep web searches on Johnson and Hanson. Both are common names in Minnesota and lots of possible relatives showed up. Which gave me an idea on how to broaden the search for Stinky.

I pressed numbers and got Jim again.

"Haven't heard from him, Harry."

"Okay. Thanks. Just checking on his name."

"His name?"

"Yeah. He only wants cash, so we pay him in cash. You pay him by check?"

"I do. He's on my payroll. Taxes, you know."

"I do. What's his full name?"

"Just a minute." Jim did some checking, came back, and said, "John James Johnson." He also gave me Stinky's Social Security Number.

"Thanks, Jim." He told me don't mention it and we ended the call.

I plugged the info into the search engine and let it crawl through the deep web. When it finished spitting back results, I looked over the list of possible relatives. One name jumped out at me. Bonnie Johnson. Could our Bonnie Johnson and our Stinky be related? Possibly. If they are, what does the one know about the other? One a private gumshoe and the other a suspected murderer. Or is that murderess? Anyway, I'll pass the info on to Tina and she can sort it out.

That little task done, I went to the kitchen. Bea had made tea. I poured myself a cup. She informed me breakfast was ready in case I wanted to eat. There was an omelet, toast, hash browns, bacon, and a fruit salad. I helped her carry the food into the dining room.

"I have class," she said. "Do you need me today?"

"I don't think so."

"Okay. I have to eat and run, then."

"You sure you have to go to class?"

"Yes. I can't get recertified without going to class."

"You sure you want to be a teacher?"

"I liked teaching, Harry. Yes. I want to teach again."

"You wouldn't rather be my sex slave or something?"

She laughed out loud. A little tinkling sound. "Is that an offer I can't refuse?"

"I'm hoping."

"I don't think you're making enough to support me in the style you want me to be accustomed to."

"How much do you want?" Tina's voice startled us. She was standing in the doorway, smirk on her face. Apparently she'd heard us.

Bea looked at the ceiling, then looked at Tina. "At least eighty thousand to start. Plus benefits, of course."

I countered, "Sex slaves get benefits, but they don't get paid."

"However, receptionists do," Tina said.

Bea and I looked at each other and then looked at Tina. Together we said, "What?"

Tina continued, "Eighty thousand, though, is a bit steep. But you could be my receptionist. That would free up Harry to do more legwork. Think about it."

Bea stammered, "Uh, okay, I, I will."

"I'm passing on info," I said.

Tina waited for me to continue.

"Stinky and Bonnie might be related."

"Really?"

I nodded. "Common names. But their names show up in each other's deep web searches."

She smiled. "Thanks, Harry."

"You're welcome."

"Gotta run," Bea said. She kissed me goodbye and was off.

Tina thought a moment and said, "She's blossoming."

"She is. Tons of potential there. You serious?"

"About the job offer? Yes."

"All in the family, eh?"

"Something like that." Tina then buried herself in her iPad while munching on a bacon strip. I poured her a cup of tea and read the paper.

Cal telephoned while I was on page six. He told me we'll see Hanson at her studio at eleven and Johnson at home at four. I conveyed the info to Tina, who said she also wanted to take another look at Copley's gallery. Cal was okay with her request and rang off.

"He'll pick us up at ten-thirty," I said.

Tina nodded.

"Want me to postpone the trip downtown to the courthouse to check on Nyquist?"

She nodded again.

We remained at breakfast until Cal arrived and then we were on our way to Northeast Minneapolis. Libby

Hanson's studio is in a converted warehouse on California Street. The building is next to a line of railroad tracks. A restaurant occupies the south end of the ground floor. The rest of the space is devoted to studios for artists. We got out of Cal's Ford, entered the building, and took the stairs to the third floor.

Ms. Hanson was waiting for us. Her studio was one of five on the floor and appeared to be the largest. Three easels and a table, along with a half dozen chairs and several flat-drawer filing cabinets constituted the furniture. There were shelves and cupboards on one wall, paintings covered two and shared space with the windows on the remaining wall.

Cal made introductions and Libby invited us to sit.

Tina began by saying, "Once upon a time I owned an art gallery."

Libby was impressed. "Really? Why did you give it up?"

"Problems with my business partner."

"That's too bad," Libby sympathized, "but it happens."

"It does indeed. I'd have been open to your work. I don't do photo- or hyperrealism myself, but I find the movement fascinating."

"You paint?" Libby's voice was redolent with surprise.

"Yes. My preferred schools are Tonalism, American Impressionism, Ashcan, and Precisionism. Also early abstract in the manner of Picasso's Le *pigeon aux petit pois*."

"I don't ever recall seeing any of your work."

Tina smiled. "That's because I sell fakes."

Libby's eyes grew large and round. "You mean like forgeries?"

"I suppose you could say that. But I don't pretend they're original."

"Oh, that's good," Libby said. She paused and asked, "So why are you a detective?"

Tina shrugged. "I like the work."

"You weren't successful as a painter?"

"I was very successful. The business end soured me."

"Oh, yes, I can see that."

Cal cleared his throat.

"I guess we'd best get to business," Tina said.

"Yes, I suppose so," Libby replied. "I gave a statement to the police."

"You did. I have a few more questions to ask," Tina replied.

"Go ahead."

"For the record, my record, where were you when Jared Copley was murdered?"

"Here."

"I suppose there's no one to corroborate?"

"Haley, down the hall, was throwing pots for part of the time I was here."

Tina nodded. "Which part of the time you were here?"

"I think she left around eight."

"And when did you leave?"

"Around ten."

"Tell me about Randy Hedgeman."

"What do you want to know?"

"About your relationship with him."

"We saw each other for six, seven months and moved on."

"You didn't live together?"

"No."

"What precipitated the breakup?"

"I got tired of dealing with Randy's insecurities. It's not my fault I'm a better artist than he is."

"I suppose not. God's, if anyone's."

Libby smiled at that.

Tina went on, "Was he upset?"

"Yes. Blamed Jared."

"Was Copley to blame?"

"No. Like I said, I grew tired of him berating me. His painting sucks. It's not my fault."

"Did you and Copley copulate?"

Libby snickered. "Yes. Copley and I copulated. Several times. But he wasn't really interested in me. The one he really had the hots for was Linda Wimbly. Pretty disheartening when he shoots and says, 'Oh, God, Linda', and your name is Libby."

Tina nodded. "Yeah. That would suck."

"I knew then we weren't going anywhere and I told him so. He said he was sorry and understood and hoped I'd still let him sell my paintings."

"Which you did."

"Sure. Put food on the table and paint on the brush."

Tina nodded. "Any thoughts on who might've killed Copley?"

"Not really. All I know is I'm screwed if I don't find another gallery."

Tina looked at the paintings on the walls. "You could try Graham's in New York or Betty Smith in San Francisco or both. Give them my name when you contact them."

Libby's eyes were saucers. "You know them?"

"Yes. Graham's is the better of the two. Once got me a six figure sale."

"You're shitting me."

"No." Tina held out a card, which Libby got up and took from her. "Tell them they can call if they need corroboration."

"Thank you, Justinia. Man." Libby, still standing, hugged Tina.

"You're welcome. If you think of anything else, let me know."

"I will."

We stood and left. On the way down the stairs, Cal said, "Six figures?"

"Yes," Tina replied.

"What the hell are you doing being a private eye?"

"I guess I like the work better than painting."

Cal shook his head. "If I could throw a little paint on a canvas and get six figures for it, I sure as hell wouldn't be a cop."

"It's all in who you know. Eric Hebborn became one of the best art forgers ever because the art world didn't appreciate his work. So he took to painting in the style of the old masters. Once Colnaghi declared his fakes genuine, Hebborn became rich. Maybe if Colnaghi had been my agent I'd still be painting for a living."

"But you had your own gallery," Cal said.

"Partner trouble."

"So you said." There was some silence and then, going through the door to the parking lot, Cal continued. "I'm really glad you came to Minneapolis and became a gumshoe."

Tina put her arm through his and said, "Me, too."

Back in Cal's Ford, we drove downtown, ate lunch at Brit's, and when done walked over to Copley's art gallery.

"Wonder what Widow Copley is going to do with the place?" Tina asked.

"Don't know. She didn't say," Cal replied. He unlocked the door and we entered.

The gallery is on the 6th Street side of Capella Tower, and on street level. Large windows allow passersby to view most of the artwork for sale. Tina went to Copley's office which also had a window on the street, which was covered by blinds and heavy drapery.

"Cal, where's the painting that was behind the desk?"

"Don't know, Tina. I don't think anyone from the department's been here since the initial phase of our investigation."

"Let's see if anything else is missing."

We looked through the gallery and Tina said the place looked as it did when she saw it before. "Curious. Very curious," she said.

"Maybe Heidi took it," I said.

"Call her and find out," Tina replied.

I called Heidi Copley. She picked up on the fourth ring.

"Mrs. Copley, this is Harry Wright."

"Hello, Mr. Wright."

"We're at the art gallery and wondering if you removed anything? There seems to be a picture missing from the office."

"No. I haven't been there. Somebody must have a key."

"Right. Somebody must. Do you plan on selling the gallery?"

"I don't know. Warren says we should keep it and hire someone to run it."

"Do you have anyone in mind?"

"No."

"Thanks for the information, Mrs. Copley. Goodbye."

She responded in kind. I ended the call and gave Cal and Tina Heidi's side of the conversation.

"Somebody has a key," Tina said. "I wouldn't be surprised to find out all of Copley's lovers have keys."

"We'll have the surveillance cameras checked," Cal said.

Tina nodded. She looked at the lone Hedgeman painting and the Hanson hanging next to it. She stood for several minutes looking from one to the other. Finally she said, "Hedgeman by a nose. Okay, I'm done here."

We left, Cal locked up, and we walked to his car. "The Johnson woman next," he said.

Bonnie Johnson owns a small house several blocks from Stinky, one of those from a bygone era when people spent most of their time outdoors and the house provided a place to sleep and cook meals. She answered the door when Cal rang the doorbell and let us come in. He made introductions and Bonnie invited us to sit.

I looked at her and smiled when she looked at me. She smiled back. A bottle blond and Walmart shopper. That's how I characterized her. Definitely working class. Like Bea. But whereas Bea had higher aspirations, to me it was clear Bonnie had no aspirations. Just go to work and pay the bills and get in some fun when you can. Dream about winning the lottery or getting a sugar daddy. In Bonnie's case, she came close to the latter.

"What do you want?" She wasn't hostile or friendly. Wary might be a good description.

"I'd like to ask a few questions," Tina said. "For starters, when did you last see Jared Copley?"

She thought a moment. "Four days before he died."

"Tell me about it."

"What's to tell. He came over before I left for work. We did our thing and then he left."

"You're not an artist."

"No."

"So why Copley?"

"Why not? He liked me and I liked him. He gave me things and money."

Tina nodded. "Why not, as you say." Tina thought a moment. "You ever meet Linda Wimbly?"

Bonnie shook her head. "Who's that?"

"One of Copley's many lovers. One he seemed very fond of."

Fire flashed in Bonnie's eyes and then she got it under control. "He fucked a lot of women. But we were going away together. To Mexico." She looked triumphant.

"Did you know he and Linda Wimbly had plans to meet at a motel the night he died?"

"That's a lie. He said he was done with that bitch."

"So you know of the Wimbly woman."

Bonnie knew she flubbed it. "Yeah, I knew about her. He told me it was over with her and we were going to Mexico. He was leaving his wife. That's what he told me."

"And you believed him?"

"Sure. He told me he loved me."

Tina nodded. "If he loved you, why was he meeting Linda Wimbly?"

"How would I know? Maybe the bitch is making it up. He told me he was through with her."

Tina sat in thought.

I asked, "Do you happen to know a John Johnson? Goes by the nickname, 'Stinky'?"

"Yeah. He's my cousin. Why?"

"He's working for us and just disappeared."

"Probably stoned."

"When was the last time you saw Stinky?" I asked Bonnie.

"I don't know. A couple months ago? We weren't close."

Tina asked if she could use Bonnie's bathroom. Bonnie told her she could and how to get to it.

I asked, "Did you feel out of place not being an artist?"

"At first, maybe," Bonnie said. "But Jared said that is what he liked about me. I wasn't an artist. Just a plain, honest person."

I nodded and was going to ask another question when Tina came back. She said to Bonnie, "Thank you."

Bonnie nodded and told her she was welcome.

Tina asked, "Copley ever give you any paintings?"

"No."

"Then why is the one from his office in your bedroom?"

Bonnie jumped up. "You bitch! What were you doing in my bedroom?"

Cal stood and Bonnie sat down.

"I think we're done. You can leave." Bonnie was fuming.

Cal said, "We can continue talking here, or I can take you downtown."

Bonnie stared daggers at Tina and then Cal. She even tossed a couple my way. In the end, she decided there's no place like home. She said, "He told me if anything happened to him, that painting was my ticket."

"I doubt it," Tina said. "The painting has no value."

"What do you mean?"

"Just what I said. The painting might fetch a few hundred dollars."

"You're lying. He said..." Her jaw was working but no sound came out of her mouth.

"The painting is by an unknown artist and is a generic scene. Sorry, but it's not your ticket to ride."

"That lying sack of shit. He told me...," she didn't continue.

"What did he tell you?" Tina asked.

"The painting would make me set. If anything happened to him, he said, 'Take the painting'. And he gave me a key to the gallery." She buried her face in her hands. "The bastard. The lying bastard."

Tina said, "I think we're done for now. Don't do anything with the painting just yet."

Cal jumped in. "Yes. It's part of a criminal investigation. In fact, I'm going to take it with us. Possible evidence."

Bonnie was despondent. "Whatever."

Tina and Cal got the painting and we all went out to the car. Cal put the picture in the trunk. On the way back to Tina's, Cal said, "And?"

"You know. The goose that laid the golden eggs?"

Cal uttered a very hesitant, "Yeah?"

"She killed it."

"She did, eh?"

"Yes. And you better have your boys check out Stinky's house. I doubt he's breathing anymore."

I chimed in, "I caught that. She said she and Stinky weren't close instead of aren't close."

"I got that, too," Cal said. "But what's with the picture?"

"I'll show you when we get home. Harry?"

"Yes, Sis?"

"Get all three. We need to find who Stinky talked to and what he or she told him."

I took out my phone and started making calls. By the time we were through downtown, I'd spoken with them. To Tina, I said, "Ed and Gwen will start right away. David's on his way back from Chicago. He got a lot of info, but nothing that will finger Asner."

"Because he didn't do it," she replied.

Cal pulled up in front of our place. Bea's car was in the driveway. He got the picture from the trunk and we went inside.

Bea came to see who'd come in. "Hi guys!" she said and came over to give me a kiss. "I have supper almost ready."

Tina said to Cal, "Stay?"

"Sure. Why not?" he replied

Tina indicated we should go to the office. Bea started for the kitchen and Tina said, "You, too, Bea. If the food can spare your attention."

"Sure. Thanks."

"Lay the picture there on the table, Cal, with the back up," Tina said.

Cal did so and said, "If the painting is worthless, was Copley just being a jerk?"

"We'll see in a minute," Tina replied. She examined the back, went to her desk, and came back with a knife. She carefully worked the knife around the back of the picture until the panel came loose. "Now we'll see if he was a lying sack of shit or not." She removed the back.

"Oh, my God!" Bea exclaimed.

The painting had been done on a canvas stretched over a wooden frame and then a false back attached. Secured to the false back were packs of hundred dollar bills and Ziploc bags of jewelry and gemstones.

Tina laughed. "Apparently he never told her the secret of the painting. In a way, he was a jerk."

"How'd you know?" Cal asked.

"I ran a gallery. I used the same technique. Deal in cash and avoid the taxes."

Cal looked at her. "You're shitting me."

"Wish I was. Those weren't my most ethical days. The shit you do for love. And that's what we have here. Murder for love and profit."

Cal nodded. "It's falling into place."

"Yes," Tina said. "As soon as we find the person Stinky talked to, the puzzle will have all the pieces in place."

"I best check on supper," Bea said.

"I'll help," I volunteered and left the office with Bea while Cal made a phone call.

"So, Harry, is it solved?" Bea asked.

"Pretty much," I replied. "We just need to gather the last bits of evidence. What do you need help with?"

"I'm almost done with the salad. Would you put the side vegetable on to cook?"

"Sure, Babe."

"Do you like this investigation work, Harry?"

"It's okay. Can be very boring or very exciting or anything in between."

"Would you like me working here?"

"It's not what I want, Bea, it's what you want. I thought you liked teaching."

"I did. But I like what I see here."

"Tina can be a crank."

"I see that, but I had her all wrong. She's nothing like Alicia. She's not fake and she's really caring." Tears were running down her cheeks and her voice was catching. "I mean, she, um, a, just, you know, let me stay, and, you know, made me feel welcome, and, I mean, like you, she's been so nice to me and—" She broke off crying.

"Oh, Babe." I took her in my arms and held her tightly against me. "Don't feel you have to take Tina's offer. Do what you think you'll be happiest doing."

"Okay, Harry." She wiped her eyes and her hand came away all black. "Damn makeup. I suppose I look like the Bride of Frankenstein."

"Nope. Your hair is normal."

"Gee. Thanks." She went to the bathroom and came back a few minutes later sans makeup.

She finished the salad and I made a dressing while the side vegetable steamed. When everything was done, we hauled the food into the dining room and I called Tina and Cal.

"You want wine, Bea?"

"You know, Harry, I'm really a beer girl. I drank wine to make Alicia happy. But I'd rather have a beer."

"Okay. So will Cal. He likes Leinie's. Okay for you?"

"Do you have Old Milwaukee or Schell's?"

"Schell's? Huh. Let me check."

"Pabst or Stroh's is also good."

I disappeared into the basement, checked the beer fridge and came back up. "None of those. We have Sam Adams, Leinie's, Bass, Guinness, and a couple of German beers."

"Leinie's Original, then."

"Got it, for you and Cal. Zinfandel for Tina and I."

The meal was delicious. Pork chops baked in tomatoes, potatoes, and sauerkraut. Fine cut broccoli florets, cauliflower, and kale with thyme and rosemary. And a tossed salad with homemade honey-mustard dressing. I just might lose my job as chief.

"So you're a down home gal, eh, Bea?" Cal said, raising his beer glass to her.

"You bet," she said, all smiles, and raised hers in response.

"Beer's okay for hamburgers and hotdogs," Tina said, "but real food needs wine."

"I didn't know you were French, Wright," Cal said.

"I'm not. English."

"Then you ought to be drinking beer with Bea and I."

"Why do you think the English imported wine? Because beer sucks."

"Really now. Only those Norman French aristocrats drank wine. The real English, the Anglo-Saxons, they drank — and drink — beer."

I like Norm. But he doesn't hold a candle to Cal, who's the only one who can and will go toe to toe with Tina. Sure wish they'd get married. The rest of the supper-time entertainment consisted of part two of the Cal and Tina show. Bea and I chuckled and played footsie under the table. When we'd cleaned our plates, we retired to the living room and Bea served tea and cookies.

Cal had taken a bite of a ginger snap when his phone rang. We listened and his side didn't sound good. When he ended the call, he said, "I have to go. We broke into Stinky's house. He's dead."

"I thought so," Tina said. "Check his cheeks for DNA in case she kissed him."

Cal nodded.

Bea covered her mouth with her hand.

I just shook my head. Not fair. Life just isn't fair.

Tina walked with Cal to the front door and returned in a few minutes. She drank her tea and when finished, excused herself. She left the room and a few minutes later we heard the sound of Philip Glass's "Metamorphosis Two" come from the piano. The somewhat sad mood of the music was fitting.

VII - Tuesday, 24 September

GWEN POISSON CALLED IN three minutes before noon. "I found her and I got her to tell me what she told Stinky."

"What's her name?" I asked.

"Gladys Kravinski."

"Address?"

Gwen gave me the address and said, "I'll be at your place ASAP."

I called Cal and told him what Gwen had discovered. He said he wanted to hear her report and was on his way.

Cal arrived a good twenty minutes before Gwen. Helps to have a siren and flashing lights. When Gwen arrived, I made sure there was lemonade and canapés for those who were hungry since we were meeting at lunchtime.

Gwen took a glass of lemonade, ate a mushroom and olive canapé, and began. "I talked with Mrs. Gladys Kravinski for about twenty-five minutes. She's a widow, lost a son in Vietnam, and is pretty disgusted with how the city has 'gone to hell in a handbasket.'" Gwen making quote marks in the air with her fingers around the phrase "gone to hell in a handbasket."

Gwen continued, "Mrs. Kravinski said a nice young man had come to talk with her about Mr. Copley's murder. Mrs. Kravinski let me know she keeps an eye on everything that happens on their street. In her words, 'Somebody has to'. So imagine my surprise when she hauls out a pair of Zeiss binoculars and night vision goggles! I asked her where she got them and she said, 'Why online, of course. Just because I'm eighty-five doesn't mean I don't know how to use a computer'. Then in a hushed voice she said, 'I even know how to search the deep web'. And then she winked at me!"

"Maybe we should hire Mrs. Kravinski to head up our crime watch program," Cal said. "So what did she see?"

"I don't think so, Cal," Gwen said. "She thinks the police are part of the problem."

Cal rolled his eyes. Tina snickered.

Gwen continued. "Mrs. K is good. She has a notebook on just the Copleys. She thinks he's Mafia — in Italy — Copliano being his real name, or something like that — and he's an art smuggler. On the date Copley was murdered, she has the time he left in the morning, times for Mrs. Copley's two morning excursions, the time Asner showed up, that he and Heidi loaded his car with boxes, the time they left, the time Jared Copley returned home, and the time Heidi and Asner returned. She also has the time the first squad car showed up."

"Any of that differ from what we have on record?" Cal asked.

"No. Not that it would make much difference," Gwen responded.

Tina spoke. "But there's more."

Gwen smiled. She has a very pretty smile. Wonder why I never noticed that before. Gwen continued, "While Heidi and Asner were loading boxes into Asner's car, Mrs. K noticed a white Pontiac slowly driving down the street. She wasn't able to catch the license plate number or the model."

I said, "Doesn't Bonnie have a white Pontiac?"

Cal said, "Yes."

Gwen continued. "The car stopped at the intersection and turned right. Then about ten minutes later the car showed up again, but this time drove through the intersection and parked. Mrs. K got the number and the model. A Pontiac Grand Prix." Gwen read the license plate number to Cal. He wrote it down and called it in.

She continued, "When Heidi and Asner left, so did the Pontiac. And that's that. Mrs. K thinks whoever was driving the Pontiac parked on a different street, came back, and broke into Copliano's house — her words — and killed him."

"Why didn't she give this information to the police?" Cal asked.

"Because the police are in the Mafia's pocket, Cal." Gwen was all smiles.

"Good God," he said.

"She's glad 'one more Mafioso' is dead."

"Jesus Christ," Cal muttered. "She said that?"

Gwen nodded.

He shook his head. "Fruitcakes. The world is full of them. Why'd she give this to Stinky?"

"Because he spoke some Polish to her when he found out her name," Gwen said.

"Why'd she speak to you?"

"Because I told her he got killed and we're trying to find out who killed him. She nodded when I said that and whispered to me 'The Mafia' and then told me what I told you."

Cal sighed. "Looks like this one is a wrap. Good work, Gwen."

"Thanks, Cal."

"Catch you all later. Gotta murderer to apprehend."

Cal left. I paid Gwen cash and she left. When I returned to my desk, Tina had a cigar going, La Gloria Cubana, and was drinking a glass of madeira. Not the 1952 vintage Malmsey, however.

"What about the painting?" I asked.

"I suppose it goes to Widow Copley."

"What about Norm?"

"I don't know. It's nice to have Cal back, though."

I smiled. "That it is."

VIII - Saturday, 5 October

TINA, NORM, BEA, AND I were sitting at the dining room table. Breakfast was mostly over. Tina was her usual non-communicative self. Norm, Bea, and I chatted about events in the newspaper. When the doorbell rang at ten, I was puzzled and voiced my wonder at who would be visiting us just before ten on a Saturday morning. I went to the door and imagine my surprise when I saw Cal on the step. Talk about a dilemma. I opened the door.

"Hi, Cal."

"Hey, Major." He had flowers in his left hand. "Tina home?"

"Uh, yes. Go on into the office and I'll get her."

Cal paused and the look on his face indicated he was thinking to ask a question. Then decided not to and went on into the office.

I went to the dining room and told Tina she had a client in the office. She gave me a questioning look. I ran the fingers of my right hand through my hair and said, "All the way from downtown and it's important."

Tina nodded and said, "Okay, if it's important." She stood, gave Norm a peck on the cheek and walked to the office.

Norm looked at me. "Does she really have a client?"

"Yes," I replied. "We work pretty much twenty-four seven, unless of course we're not working, which we aren't at the moment, but we have to always be ready because when people want our services it is usually a crisis. At least a crisis for them."

Norm nodded and went back to his section of the paper. A half-hour later Tina rejoined us.

"Cal said—"

"Wait a minute," Norm interrupted, "I thought you said you had a client."

"Cal is our client," I explained. "He hired us, the department actually, as consultants."

Norm was none too happy with my answer.

Tina continued, "Cal said Bonnie attempted to flee. Managed to shake off her watchers here and was heading south, probably for Mexico. She tried to out run the Texas State Patrol and ended up in a high speed chase. She lost control of her car and ran it off the road. It flipped over and landed in a ravine. She didn't survive."

"And so ends another case," I said.

"And so it does," Tina replied.

Norm looked at his watch. "I need to run. Have a few errands." He and Tina rose and left the dining room. But she was back in a few minutes.

"What was with the flowers?" I asked.

"Flowers? Cal brought you flowers?" Bea said.

Tina nodded.

"And?" Bea was all excited about the flowers.

"I don't know what to do."

Bea and I looked at each other. Tina rarely admits she doesn't know what to do. Even when she doesn't have a clue, she makes you think she does.

"What do you mean?" Bea asked.

"The Copley case got me thinking. So many unhappy people looking for some manner of happiness. I look at you two and I look at myself. Cal told me he loves me and hopes we can patch up whatever it is that keeps us apart. He said, 'I know you're seeing someone and if you don't want to leave him I'll accept it. But we're good, you and I'. And he's right." Her eyes took in Bea and I and then she walked out of the dining room.

A few minutes later we heard the piano sound the notes of Warlock's "Pavane." A lonely and mournful piece, in my opinion.

"She's hurting, Harry," Bea said.

"Yeah. I know. They need to get married."

Fingers touched keys and Warlock's "Pavane" played on.

Bottom Line

1 - Monday, 2 December

SNOW WAS FALLING. I could see the stuff coming down in great big flakes. Tina was doing her best to talk Deloris Delia Anderson out of hiring her, without flatly refusing, and Deloris was doing her best to talk Tina into taking the job.

We'd been busy since Cal reappeared on the scene back in September. Two industrial espionage cases, four missing person cases, we tracked down a stolen painting, and gathered evidence for a defense attorney to get his very guilty client off on a technicality. And somewhere in and amongst all of that Tina rehearsed the Arthur Foote Piano Quintet with the Hamlin University string quartet and performed a recital at the beginning of November. She let the students keep the one thousand one hundred and eighty-seven dollars in donations.

Bea accepted Tina's offer to become our receptionist, which meant a little remodeling had to be done to the old mansion to create a waiting room and a place for Bea to work. About the only change in our routine is Bea now answers the door and phone most of the time and has taken on a good share of our official paperwork.

Throughout October and November Tina had little time to pursue anything with Cal or Norm. Both were left dangling on the string. Both showed up at the recital, which wasn't the most comfortable. I think she's seeing which one loses steam and drops out of the race first. I converted one of the spare bedrooms into the official gift room because she's acquiring quite a few. Although the first one to deliver a 1955 Thunderbird or a 1937 Pierce-Arrow Metropolitan Town Brougham, or a new Bugatti Veyron or Lamborghini Veneno will certainly win the prize. And if either one really loved her, they might consider a 1933 Pierce Silver Arrow or a Hennessey Venom GT. If they come through, we'll need an addition to the garage.

But back to Delores Delia Anderson. Tina finally resorted to the tried-and-true technique of getting rid of potential clients by setting an outrageous fee. "Very well Ms. Anderson. If you want personal protection — which is not my agency's specialty—"

"But you're the best," Deloris interrupted. "Everyone says so."

"At what we do, yes," Tina replied, "but if you want personal protection it will cost you one thousand per hour and fifteen thousand for the surveillance and alarm equipment."

Ms. Anderson's mouth opened and stayed that way. No sound came out. I wasn't sure if she was simply in shock, trying to think of a polite way to tell Tina she was full of shit, or might actually be considering the offer. Much like a movie scene in slow motion we sat there, no one moving or saying anything. Than slowly Deloris Anderson closed her mouth, swallowed, licked her lips, paused, and finally said, "Okay. How do I pay you?"

"I'll take the fifteen thousand now. We'll bill you each month for the hours we put in. Harry, give Ms. Anderson a contract."

"Do you accept a credit card?" she asked.

"We do," I said. "To cover the fee, we'll need another four hundred and fifty dollars."

Ms. Anderson shook her head and gave me her Visa in exchange for the contract. She read it over and signed it. "I see you make no guarantees."

"Of course not," Tina said. "A resourceful killer can always find a way. But I will do the best I and my people can to protect you. But in case of your demise, you do agree to hold us harmless unless your heirs can prove gross negligence on our part."

"How soon will you start?" she asked.

Tina looked at the clock. "It's two twenty-seven now. Harry?"

"I'll follow you home and while doing so will make phone calls. Everything should be rolling by the time we reach your place."

"Very well. But I'd rather you ride with me."

I shrugged my shoulders. "Alright. I'm ready when you are."

Ms. Anderson and I left the office. Bea was at the reception desk and I told her I was working and would see her when I saw her. Then our client and I were out the front door and getting into her BMW M3 Coupe.

"Nice car," I told her and she smiled a rather arrogant smile. The kind that says, bet you can't afford one. And I can't, but then I'm not into cars. Even though I have a Maserati, courtesy of Bea and a dead Alicia Harris. My Focus wagon works just fine. Although I may have to drive the Maserati the next time I'm on duty for Ms. Anderson.

She pulled into the underground parking at the North Star Lofts. Bea looked at getting a loft in the old converted textile building, but decided the price was too high. They go for as much as two million. Although the poorer wealthy can pick one up for a mere third of a mil. Wouldn't want the high-priced spread thinking the hoi polloi were coming to ask for a handout.

Deloris Delia Anderson is Senior Account Executive with Catchfire, Inc. According to her, she has turned Catchfire around and made it into one of the fastest growing ad agencies in Minnesota. She earns her six figure income and you better believe it. But in the past three weeks she has gotten the feeling someone is stalking her. Phone calls and no one responding when she says hello. The feeling she's being watched during her morning fitness walk. Then, yesterday, someone knocked her down when she was about a half-mile into her five and a half mile walk. That was the last straw.

"I'm afraid," she told Tina. "I'm afraid someone wants to hurt me or kill me."

Tina had explained to her the simple fact of life that if someone wanted her dead, only God could truly stop the person. And only if the Deity chose to do so.

But Ms. Anderson had insisted. Tina asked about enemies and with a bitter laugh Deloris Anderson cataloged a long list of folks who might have reason to wish her dead. In her climb up the corporate ladder, she had not followed Dale Carnegie's advice. Nor had she in her personal affairs.

Tina phrased the sentence more politely, but it boiled down to, "You're screwed, Lady."

Nevertheless, Tina ended up taking the case even though she didn't want it and made sure Deloris Anderson knew of her displeasure by draining Deloris's wallet of some of her hard earned cash.

Deloris's loft is truly something. Spacious and airy. Beautiful view of the city through great, big windows. More beautiful views from a balcony. A private rooftop cabana to enjoy the summer air and the stars at night.

When we entered, barking, whining, and a wagging tail greeted us. "Buddy is my best friend," Deloris said. Then with a bitter laugh, added, "Who am I kidding. He's my only friend." The little affenpinscher sure seemed to like her.

She mixed herself a martini. I shook my head when she offered me one. Deloris sat on a couch by one of her fireplaces. Not real, of course. A fake, gas burning pseudo-fireplace. I told her I was going to look around. She took a sip of her drink and waved her hand, indicating I was free to go ahead.

There wasn't much to see. Only eighteen hundred square feet. Essentially one gargantuan room sectioned off into kitchen, living room, and dining room spaces. The two bedrooms constituted the other rooms. Laundry was located behind doors in an alcove. The only way in or out was through the door. Unless our murderer climbed up six floors to the balcony, or dropped down from the roof. Might be a better way to go, since the building is only seven floors. Provided, of course, our potential assassin could get there undetected loaded down with rappelling equipment. Nevertheless, alarms for windows and balcony door seemed appropriate. She already had an alarm for her main door.

There's building security, too. In looking over the set up, I didn't think she had much to worry about provided she never left the building. The possibility always existed for the potential hit man or woman to gain entrance masquerading as a delivery person, repair person, inspector, any number of ways, which was Tina's point and why she didn't want the case. But to my eye, the building looked pretty secure. The danger lay in when Deloris Anderson left the confines of her protective womb. And for that we needed people.

On the trip to Ms. Anderson's luxury condo, I'd called our friends at the Three Sisters Agency. Melissa Olson and her younger twin sisters, Helen and Heloise, run a pretty top drawer security service. I'd asked her if she had anyone available.

"Sure, Harry," Melissa had said. "I have an ex-Army Ranger and an ex-Marine who could use some work."

Melissa and I talked about the situation and she thought her ex-military people would fit the bill. I asked her to send them over to see if they'd pass our clients muster and she said she would right away. They arrived within half an hour of our arrival. I went down to greet them in the lobby.

Logan Arneson is a twenty-five year career Army veteran who saw duty in Iraq and has been in the security business for five years. He's forty-eight. Jazmin Washington is thirty-six and served in the Marines for ten years and has been in the security business for eight. Deloris thought they would be fine. She explained her routine to them and we formulated a security plan.

My part in the overall scheme of things done, I called into the office and asked Bea to pick me up. She said she or Tina would be there shortly. I took the elevator down to the lobby. A few minutes later, Logan and Jazmin, with Deloris, were in the lobby and then departed for a look in the garage and to talk to building security. My cell rang and I answered it. Tina was waiting on Portland in the Crossfire. I joined her and we were on our way home.

I gave her a summary of my findings and who we had working on the case. Tina nodded and sighed. After a moment she said, "She's dead, you know."

"She is?"

"If whoever is stalking her seriously wants to kill her."

"If they're serious. Maybe they just want to scare her."

"Maybe. My money says she's dead by New Year's."

"Really."

Tina nodded.

I thought it over. "Okay. Hamilton says you're wrong."

"Might as well give it to me now."

"Nothing doing. She was breathing the last time I saw her."

Tina shrugged. "Suit yourself."

"By the way, anything special you want for Christmas?"

She thought a moment. "Not really. Surprise me with something luxurious."

I smiled. "Okay, Sis. Something luxurious coming up in twenty-three days."

"And you?"

"Let's see. Can always use stamps."

"How many games do you have going?"

"By mail, I'm in two tournaments. Eighteen games. Internet? Around thirty."

"I'd rather play chess face to face."

"That's because you like to watch them suffer."

She laughed. "Intellectual BDSM."

I shook my head. "God. Only you would come up with that."

"Anything besides stamps?"

"Not really. You know what I like."

"Ha. Not sure anymore about that since you got involved with a skinny woman."

"Geez. I'm the same old brother you've always known and loved."

"Yeah, I know. I'm just giving you crap. So stamps and the rest is up to me. Okay. What are you getting Bea?"

"Don't know. I'm kind of stumped. She doesn't want anything."

"Know what you mean. Very contented. She has you and life is wonderful."

"You getting Cal anything or Norm?"

"I don't know. Probably should."

"Yes. You probably should."

She pulled into the driveway and parked the car in the garage.

We walked into the house together. Tina went to the office and I detoured to the kitchen. Bea had something going in the crock pot and in the oven. I made tea and went on to the office. Bea was at her desk. A smile lit up her face when she saw me. "You're back!" she said.

"I am indeed, Buttercup." I gave her a kiss. "Been quiet?"

"Very."

"You can knock off, if you want. I'll watch the phone and door."

"That's okay. I can do what I'm doing here as well as anywhere else."

"What are you doing?"

"Tatting."

"Really? Didn't know anybody did that anymore."

"I do. My grandmother taught me."

"Good. Won't become a lost art."

Bea smiled and I went on into the office. Tina was at her desk smoking a cigar and drinking madeira. I sat at mine and took a sip of tea. Decided to smoke a pipe. Chose an old bent bulldog, filled it with a good and strong McClelland latakia blend, and fired it up.

Less than a minute later, Tina looked up from her book and said, "You're smoking that latakia shit again. Good God." She stood and left the office.

That's one way to clear a room.

A half hour later Bea stuck her head in and made a face.

"God, Harry, it stinks in here. I'm going to finish up supper preparations."

I told her I loved her too.

Granted, latakia is a pungent tobacco. Many years ago a friend told me it smelled like the armpits of a hundred Armenian rug merchants after they crossed the Gobi desert, but it sure tasted good. I can attest to the latter. I have no clue about the accuracy of the former. I think it smells more like camel dung fires. Be that as it may, I love the taste. And it is good for clearing a room, which comes in handy if you want a little solitude.

My pipe smoked out, I put it aside, and ambled on to the kitchen.

"Need any help, Babe?"

"Nope, I have it under control."

"I'll set the table, then."

"Thanks, hon."

I set the table, then wandered into the library. Tina was there reading. I waved my hand to dissipate the cloud of cigar smoke.

"You aren't coming in here with that pipe."

"No."

"Good. That stuff is awful."

"Smells better than a day old cigar. Now that is what you call stench."

Bea poked her head in. "Is there a fire in here?"

I burst out laughing and Tina glowered.

Bea smiled, said, "Supper's ready," and left.

Tina put out the remnant of her cigar and drank the remainder of her glass of madeira. I followed her to the dining room. Bea had made a pot roast with potatoes, onions, and carrots in the crock pot. In the oven she'd baked a butternut squash and a mushroom stuffed eggplant. There was also a mixed lettuce and greens salad, accented with grape tomatoes, pea pods, kohlrabi, celery, and cucumber. The dressing was a simple oil and vinegar with crushed garlic, basil, and oregano.

We sat and ate. The conversation drifted from topic to topic. Then Bea wanted to know if Ms. Anderson's case was an easy one. Tina replied, "She's as good as dead."

"Oh, dear. Really?" Bea said.

"She was breathing the last time I saw her," I said. "Sis is just morbid, that's all."

"I'm not morbid," Tina replied. "Just realistic."

"Then why did you take the case?" Bea asked.

"Because she wouldn't go away and if she wants to give someone her money it might as well be me."

"But is that ethical?"

"Depends on how you define 'ethical.'"

I said, "Tina's point is simply this: there is little chance of thwarting the intention. It's simply a matter of time."

"Really?" Bea said, her eyes wide.

"I've seen it happen too many times," Tina said.

"You have?" Bea said.

Tina nodded. "CIA."

"Oh."

Tina continued, "I told her what I'm telling you and still she insisted. So—" Tina shrugged. "I took her money. We'll do our best, but against a determined murderer it's just a matter of time. This pot roast is the bomb."

Bea blushed. "Thanks."

I added, "If Ms. Anderson stayed in her secure condo she'd have a better chance at survival. But she doesn't want to do that."

"I see," Bea said.

"The eggplant is delicious, Bea," I said.

"Thanks," she replied. "Glad you like my cooking. You're a hard act to follow, Harry."

Tina said, "You're a good cook, Bea, you've nothing to be ashamed of."

"You two are so good to me. I love you."

Tina smiled and blew her a kiss.

We finished the meal and Bea wanted to know if we'd like dessert now or later. The spiced plums in port was tempting, but Tina and I both said later. Tina moved to the music room and I helped Bea with the dishes.

The phone rang. I looked to see who it was. Norm. I answered. "Hey, Norm. How're things?"

"Good, Harry. And for you?"

"Just grand."

"That's good. Tina around?"

"Sure. Hang on."

I told Tina the phone was for her and she took the call in the office.

Bea asked me, "Who do you think Tina's going to end up with?"

"Between Norm or Cal?"

She nodded.

"My money's on Cal because that's what's always happened in the past."

"I like them both. I'm glad I don't have to choose."

"Yeah. I think she likes Norm a lot and that's what's complicating things this time around. But my money is still on Cal."

"Anything in particular you want for Christmas, Harry?"

"Tina asked me the same thing. I can always use stamps. Otherwise, I'm open. I have you and I'm very satisfied."

"Thanks, Harry. That means a lot to me."

"What about you?"

There was a pause, long enough for me to wonder what was going on inside her head. Finally she said,

"Harry, I love you and I'm glad we're together. You are everything to me. The only thing I want for Christmas is a piece of paper that tells me I'm Mrs. Harry Gill Wright. I want to marry you, Harry. On Christmas Day would be wonderful, but any time will do."

Now I paused. This was it. I love Bea. Why is marrying her such an issue? If I told her I wasn't ready, I know she wouldn't go anywhere. For all intents and purposes we are married. Just not in the legal eyes of the state of Minnesota. And yet...

"Harry, it's okay if you don't want to marry me."

"Bea, it's not that. I love you. We're together and I'm very happy."

"It's okay, Harry. You have a hang-up on marriage. I know you love me and I know you won't leave me."

"But it would make you feel better."

She nodded. "You know I'm kind of insecure. I'm sorry but that stupid piece of paper will help. I'm sorry."

"No, Bea. I'm the one who's sorry. I'm kind of messing this up. There's no reason we shouldn't be married."

She kissed me. "Harry, I'll wait. I'm with you and I'm happy. I can wait until you're ready."

"I'm sorry, Bea."

"Don't be. I shouldn't press you. I'm sorry."

"No, I'm sorry."

"No, I'm sorry."

"No, me."

"Me."

And we both dissolved into laughter.

II - Friday and Saturday, 6 - 7 December

TINA AND NORM WENT to a play at the Guthrie. Bea and I stayed home and streamed a movie. I made popcorn and we drank cream soda. The fire in the fireplace was warm and cozy. Halfway through the movie, snuggled together on the couch, we began kissing. And then, well, we were naked and made love in front of the fire. Life is perfect right now with Bea. We got ourselves put back together and watched the rest of the movie, wrapped up in a blanket and each other's arms. The movie wasn't too good apparently because Tina woke us up when she came home.

"Norm here?" I asked.

"No," she replied.

"Are you okay?" Bea asked.

"I don't know," Tina said. She sat on the couch with us.

Bea reached out and took her hand. "What happened?"

"I had a wonderful time with Norm. The play was good. We had drinks after. I like him very much. Maybe I even love him."

Prudy jumped into Tina's lap and she started petting her cat.

"But I told him, this was it. I asked him not to call me anymore."

"Wow," I said.

Bea scooched over next to Tina, put her arms around her, kissed her cheek, and held her. And then Tina started crying. I can't remember the last time I saw her cry. I got up and knelt beside her and put my arms around her.

After a moment, she wiped her eyes with her hand and said, "Thanks guys, I'm okay." She fished in her purse for her cell phone. When she found it, she told it to call "Cal".

"Tina, it's two in the morning," I said.

"I know. There's a clock on this thing." The phone was ringing, but he wasn't picking up. Suddenly she said, "Swenson, are you coming over?" A pause. "Yes, I know it's two in the morning." Another pause. "Look, you better get your ass over here. I just put all my eggs in one basket." A somewhat lengthy pause and when Tina spoke, her voice was soft. "See you soon and, and, I love you, Cal."

The call ended and she just sat there. Bea took her hand and gave it a squeeze. Tina smiled and then the smile disappeared. "I'm scared. There's something different this time around."

"It's okay, Sis. We're here."

"Thanks."

"C'mon, Bea, we need to hit the hay."

"Sure, Harry. Goodnight Tina."

"Goodnight you two. Thanks."

Bea and I went up to my room. I suppose I should say our room, since that is what it's become. We'd just gotten into bed when the doorbell rang.

⏷

I was the first one up in the morning, or I should say later in the morning. The tea kettle was on and I was shredding potatoes for hash browns when Cal came down.

"Morning, Harry."

"Morning, Cal. Get any sleep?"

"Eventually. Can you tell me what the hell happened?"

"Not exactly, but I think she's really serious this time around."

"I kinda gathered that."

The tea kettle whistled and I poured the boiling water onto tea leaves.

"I do love her, Harry. You know that, don't you?"

"I do, Cal. For a long time, I suspect."

"From the beginning. When we first met."

"I think Tina's at the point she is willing to give a relationship with you a serious run for its money."

"Me, too. We aren't getting any younger, you know."

"And you are telling me this?"

With a smirk on his face he said, "Oh, yeah, I forgot, Gramps."

"I'll put Black Leaf 40 in your pancakes if you aren't careful."

Cal laughed and I poured us each a cup of tea.

Bea was the next one down. She wore a simple knee-length dress, belted at the waist to give a flair effect, with a puff where the sleeves meet the top to give the illusion of larger shoulders. The neckline was high and collared. The color was a bold reddish-orange.

"Hi guys!" she called out.

"How's my girl?" I asked as she came up to me and kissed my lips.

"Just fine." She gave Cal a peck on the cheek.

"Good morning, Bea," he said.

I poured her a cup of tea. We chatted and when breakfast was made, we moved into the dining room. Tina joined us just as we sat down. She was wearing blue jeans and a heavy forest green sweater and her fiery red hair was down in a bold cascade of color. Where was the suit? She always wears a skirt suit.

She muttered a good morning, gave Cal a peck on the lips, and sat down.

Cal was about to say something, thought better of it, and took a sausage instead. He poured her a cup of tea and she muttered, thanks.

I gave the newspaper to Bea and Cal. I looked over the reports from Logan Arneson and Jazmin Washington for the week as of yesterday. They reported no problems and nothing suspicious. Each day, the same boring routine. They tried to get Deloris to vary the route of her walk, but she adamantly refused to change anything. Talk about a death wish. Our client had it.

Jazmin had managed to get out of Ms. Anderson she suspected her brother to have the most animus against her. She'd stiffed him on a sizable chunk of an inheritance from an aunt. Second on Anderson's list was Ashley Morgan, with whom Anderson had a brief relationship. Anderson not only dumped Ashley, she then proceeded to get her forced out of Catchfire. Ms. Morgan, to her credit, took a huge client with her and started her own agency, Ashley and Morgan. A rather creative use of her name.

"Kind of early for business, but do we want to put tails on the two suspects Anderson finally named?" I asked Tina.

She looked up from her iPad. "Since it will cost her extra, ask her."

"Will do."

Tina went back to her iPad.

Logan and Jazmin had put in twenty hours of combined surveillance thus far. Twenty grand. Hope our client thinks she's getting her money's worth. The extra security and surveillance equipment arrived and was installed on Tuesday. Now we wait and see if anything happens.

When breakfast was over, Tina and Cal took off for parts unknown. Bea and I cleaned up the kitchen and when that chore was done, went grocery shopping but not before I asked our client if she wanted us to tail the two suspects. She said no. We ate lunch at Kramer-czuk's. I had two Polish sausages and a Cossack, Bea had a brat. We washed the sandwiches down with a draft Pilsner Urquell for me and Grainbelt Nordeast for Bea.

We went home after lunch, and while hauling in the groceries I made a comment about Tina and Cal making a day of it, since there was no evidence they'd returned from wherever they'd gone.

My sweetie said they had lost time to make up for and I had to agree.

We put the food away, started in on making supper, and that's when I spied the note taped to the tea pot. They had indeed been back to pick up clothes for Tina, because she was spending the night at Cal's place.

"Well, Babe," I said, "it's just you and me. Let's go out to eat tonight and we'll fix this for tomorrow."

She thought it a great idea and that's what we did.

III – Wednesday, 25 December

CHRISTMAS MORNING STARTED WITH a light breakfast and then the four of us opened gifts. Cal, Tina, Bea, and I. The tree had been up for a couple of weeks and the lights were on, reflecting off the ornaments. Snow was falling outside. Christmas music was playing through the sound system. We drank mimosas while we opened presents.

Bea played mistress of ceremonies, handing out everyone's gifts.

First was Tina. Bea and I gave her a whole pound of 88th Night Shincha tea. Damned expensive it was, too. Cal gave her a dozen canvases and twenty-five tubes of her favorite brand of paint.

Next was Cal. Tina gave him a heavy Irish wool sweater with a zipper front. Bea and I gave him a gift certificate so he could get some music.

I got stamps and a camel hair cardigan sweater from Bea, stamps and a bottle of absinthe from Tina, and a bottle of Drambuie and Warre's Warrior Porto from Cal.

Bea left hers for last. Tina bought her perfume and a 1940s Cloche from J. Peterman Company. Cal gave her a case of Schell's beer. When she opened my gift she took one look, said, "Oh God," and started crying. In the box, a big box, was a wedding ring and a marriage license.

"The judge will be here around noon," I said.

"How? I mean, on Christmas..." Tears were streaming down her face.

"Owes Tina a favor," I said. "You okay about it?"

"Oh, yes!" And she threw herself into my arms.

The cats, who'd been burrowing into the mounds of wrapping paper, ran into hiding.

Bea looked into my eyes and asked, "Are you sure, Harry? Really, really sure?"

"I'm sure, Bea."

"Oh, God. Please don't let this be a dream."

All of us laughed. "It's not a dream," I said.

"I'm going to be Mrs. Wright. Oh, my God. I can't believe it."

"Believe it," Tina said and added, "You are one lucky gal and he's one lucky guy."

The rest of the day was anti-climatic. Even the actual magic words the judge spoke. Bea looked at her ring every ten minutes and said, "I can't believe it." I'd thought about inviting her brother and family, but they'd booked a cruise. So it ended up just Cal and Tina as witnesses. Bea was okay with how things turned out.

At dinner, Cal asked if we were going on a honeymoon.

"I think they've already had the honeymoon," Tina quipped.

Bea giggled.

I said, "I booked a week at Brigg's Pond Bed and Breakfast in Rocheport, Missouri."

"You did what?" Tina said.

"You heard me," I replied.

"And you didn't think to clear it with me?" she responded.

"Oh, don't get your undies in a bunch, Wright," Cal said. "Let 'em have fun. I'll be around to help out if you need it."

Tina looked at him. "You mean it?"

"I do."

"Deal. No bunched undies."

Bea burst out laughing and I had a pretty big grin on my face.

Tina looked our way. "Don't you two have some fucking to do or something?"

That only made Bea laugh all the harder, to the point no sound was coming out of her. I was laughing quite heartily. Cal had a big smirk on his face and even Tina was smiling.

I think the four of us are going to get along just fine.

IV - Thursday, 2 January

WE LEFT THE DAY after Christmas at five in the morning for Missouri. We drove my wagon. The snow had stopped falling. The temperature was a balmy thirteen above and the wind was calm. We pulled into Rocheport about one-thirty, met our hostess, and settled into what would be our honeymoon digs for the next week. The temperature was forty-four in Rocheport when we arrived. Somewhat better than Minneapolis. But the wind was quite breezy and that put a chill on things.

The week went by quickly. Our hostess provided us with delicious vegetarian and vegan breakfasts. We sampled the fare at Les Bourgeois Bistro and Abigail's in Rocheport, and Shakespeare's Pizza, Main Squeeze, Flat Branch, and Beeches in Columbia. We toured wineries and I bought eight cases of wonderful Missouri wine. And we spent a lot of time simply loving each other. One of the best weeks of my life.

On the second of January, we took off for home. Snow was falling and the wind chill was three below. As bad as Minneapolis. We arrived at home just before two in the afternoon. Nine below wind chill. Yuck. Cal, Tina, and a woman were in the office.

"Welcome home," Tina said.

"Hey Harry, Bea," Cal added.

Tina came from behind her desk to give Bea and I hugs. Cal hugged Bea and shook hands with me.

Cal then introduced us to the woman. "Harry, Bea, this is my new partner Detective Nicole Nelson."

We shook hands with her. Five-six, thirtyish, blond, hourglass figure, and drop dead gorgeous. She said, in a husky, sultry voice, she was pleased to meet us.

"You in a conference?" I asked.

"We are," Tina said.

"The day after you left," Cal said, "someone knocked off Deloris Anderson and Jazmin Washington."

Bea put her hand to her mouth.

I shook my head. "You were right," I said to Tina.

Tina nodded. "Sadly so," she said.

"Want me to sit in?" I asked.

"I'll catch you up later," Tina said. "Go ahead and get unpacked."

Bea and I unloaded the car and unpacked our suitcases. Bea started washing our dirty clothes and I put the wine away. Cal and Detective Bombshell Nelson left while we were in the basement and Tina joined us.

"You have a good time?" she asked.

"We did," Bea replied, "a wonderful time. The bed and breakfast was super."

"Glad to hear it," she said. "Been busy here and not so fun."

"What's with Cal's new partner?" I asked. "She looks like she should be in a magazine instead of a uniform."

Tina laughed out loud. "That's one way to put it. She is a looker. Cal says she's pretty tough when she has to be." Tina paused, then said, "I'm glad you're back. I missed you two."

"Everything okay with Cal?" Bea asked.

"Things are good. He's been very busy. I also think Detective Blond Bomber would like to put in some one on one overtime with him, but he assures me it's the two of us from here on out. And he likes you two, which helps."

"Glad to hear it," I said.

"He's been here most nights and I like him here," Tina said, something of a faraway look in her eyes.

Finished with our basement work, we went back upstairs. I volunteered to get Chinese for supper and the ladies were in favor. I ordered online and then drove over to pick it up. This winter was gearing up to be a real bitch. The worst in a long time. When I got home I made green tea and we sat down to eat.

"So what happened to Deloris Anderson?" I asked.

Tina began, "She left home at six. Jazmin was with her. You already know how quiet everything's been since we were hired."

"Too quiet," I said. "Did they get lazy?"

"You wouldn't think so being ex-military," Tina replied, "but that's my guess. There's a witness, but he didn't get a look at the face before he was hit with a shot from a pepper spray gun."

"Pepper spray?" Bea said, "Doesn't that hurt?"

Tina nodded and said, "One hell of a lot. Cal guesses the attacker was hiding by the Hennepin Bridge where the trail cuts under it and jumped out pepper spraying Jazmin and Deloris. They had face masks on, but the attacker hit their eyes and soaked their masks. Deloris had one puncture wound through the left eye into the brain. The weapon actually went through the back of the skull."

Bea winced. "How awful."

Tina nodded. "Jazmin was kicked in the head with sufficient force to snap her neck. The assailant drove the weapon through her left temple and it came out the other side. The witness managed to call 911 on his cell phone. Of course the attacker was gone by the time any help came."

"Any idea what kind of weapon?" I asked.

"Triangular cross-section. Sharp point, but probably not sharp edges. Cal thinks a stiletto or old-fashioned bayonet."

"Makes sense," I said. I paused, excused myself, went to my personal library, and came back. "Like these," I said and set on the table two replica Renaissance stilettos.

Bea said, "Oh, my God, Harry. What do you have those for?"

"Just to have. Not very practical, since I'm not an assassin."

Tina smiled. "Yes. Probably something like this. These easy to buy?"

"Oh, sure," I replied. "Internet."

Tina continued, "Cal's trying to track sales. Nothing local. Going to be more difficult getting records from a mail order source. Show these to Cal when he shows up."

"Okay. What about suspects?" I asked.

Tina smiled. "Ah, yes, who done it? Cal hasn't said much about that. We know Deloris herself was most concerned about her brother, Ronald, and her former co-worker and paramour, Ashley Morgan. Deloris was currently seeing Dr. Benjamin Grassley, an English professor at Hamlin. So we added Grassley and his wife to the suspect list. Don't know anyone else, but that doesn't mean there isn't anyone else."

"Why isn't Cal including you in the investigation?" Bea asked.

"Not sure," Tina replied. "Might have to do with Sergeant Blond Bomber."

"Really?" Bea replied. "Why would she make a difference?"

"Stickler for the rules. Cal thinks she's also something of a troublemaker. Rumor has it she didn't get promoted last time around and she raised holy hell about discrimination. So when she was up again, they promoted her."

"Really?" Bea said. "How fair is that?"

"Not very, if true." Tina said, "But she got her promotion and Cal got saddled with her."

"Bureaucracy at its finest," I said.

"Cal's been letting the Bomber call the shots. He wants to see how she does. So far so-so." Tina looked pleased.

Bea looked puzzled. "Is he wanting her to fail?"

Tina thought a moment. "Not exactly. I think he wants her to come to the realization she isn't as smart as she thinks she is. She needs to work with the team and not play the Lone Ranger."

"Up until recently, the police force was a man's world," I said. "Still kind of is. There's a lot of animosity against women. I'm not saying Cal has any, but I do see him having a very strong sense of fairness and he might think she's playing unfairly."

Tina nodded. "Could be. Anyway, you two still happily married?"

"Very," Bea said.

"Ditto," I added.

"Glad to hear it," Tina said.

"What happened to Anderson's dog, Buddy?" I asked.

"I don't know," Tina said. "You'll have to check with Cal."

I nodded.

We finished supper. Tina even helped with putting the leftovers away and the dishes. I made tea and Tina took out a mail order fruitcake for us to have with the tea. I built a fire in the living room fireplace and we sat before it eating fruitcake, drinking tea, and watching the flames. It felt good to be home with my sister and my wife. I still find it difficult to see Bea as Mrs. Wright. She, on the other hand, has no difficulty seeing herself as Mrs. Wright.

A little after ten, Cal arrived. "God, it's cold out," he said. "No wind right now. Otherwise it'd freeze the balls off an Eskimo."

Tina said, "Maybe I better check if yours are still there."

"Not in front of the kids," he replied.

Bea started giggling and I just shook my head.

He kissed Tina and sat on the floor next to her chair. "The commander is chewing my butt on this Deloris Anderson case. I'm going to have to start moving on it."

"So move on it," Tina said.

"I can bring you in as special consultant, but I'm limited to four thousand dollars."

"Okay," Tina replied.

"You serious?"

She shrugged her shoulders. "Better in my wallet than someone else's."

"Okay. We'll go over it in the morning. I'm too tired right now."

"Would you like tea and fruitcake, Cal?" Bea asked.

"Sounds good, Mrs. Wright."

Bea sighed and floated off to the kitchen.

"You're a lucky guy, Harry, to have found a gem like her," Cal said.

"Thanks. I think so, too. And if you don't mind my saying so, even though I'm biased, you're sitting next to a gem yourself."

"I know it," he said. He looked up at Tina. "You're blushing! I've never seen you blush, Wright."

"Oh, shut up and eat your fruitcake, Swenson."

Bea was standing next to Cal holding out tea and cake for him. He laughed and told Bea thanks.

"There's more tea and fruitcake," Bea said.

"Why don't you bring it in, Babe?"

"Sure thing, Sweetie."

She was back in a minute with the tea pot and cake. I helped myself to tea and a slice of the rich cake. Bea and I cuddled together on the couch. Tina had left her chair and was sitting next to Cal on the rug before the fireplace, arms around him, head on his shoulder. I can see the four of us living together for many years in the future. One big happy family. Then again, who knows? Who knows anything about anything? Sometimes dreams are just that — dreams. And wishes are nothing more than wishes. Dreams and wishes. And reality moves on.

V – Friday, 3 January

AFTER BREAKFAST WE GATHERED in the office for an extended briefing. Even Bea sat in. The wind chill outside was a balmy nine below. The sky was grey and drear. Cal had called in to let the unit know where he was.

"Starting closest to home," he began, "Ronald Anderson has motive and he has the ability, the physical strength, to jab what we're assuming is a stiletto or bayonet with sufficient force to go through the head and punch a hole out the back of the skull. And to also kick Jazmin with sufficient force to snap her neck."

"His motive?" I asked.

"He got an inheritance from an aunt. Deloris contested it and was awarded a slice of the pie. That was a dozen years ago. He hasn't spoken to her since."

"But wouldn't he have done something sooner?" I asked.

"Not necessarily," Cal explained. "But now an uncle he's been taking care of is in hospice. Isn't expected to live out the year. Perhaps he decided to make sure there isn't a repeat of the situation with the aunt."

"Alibi?" Tina asked.

"Not ironclad. Was sleeping. His house is in St. Anthony."

"What's he do for a living?" I asked.

"Writes non-fiction for women's magazines."

"Does he make money?" Bea asked.

"Says he makes eighty grand a year."

"A decent income," I noted.

Cal nodded.

"Oh! Before I forget." I opened my desk drawer and took out my stilettos. "Here, Cal, is what the murderer might have used."

Cal came to my desk to take a look. "Yeah, something like this. Where'd you get yours?"

"Mail order company. Specializes in museum quality replicas."

Cal nodded. "Wicked weapon. Although I suppose you could say all weapons are wicked." He turned the stilettos over in his hands and them put them down.

He continued, "Next suspect is Dr. Benjamin Grassley. He and Deloris have been seen together in something of a semi-open affair for about a year. Unclear if the relationship was actually sexual. But they were certainly emotionally involved. Mrs. Grassley eventually found out about it and took still longer to decide she didn't like it. Apparently Dr. Grassley broke it off, although Deloris wasn't going easily. The good doctor could have stuck a knife in Deloris to make her go more easily than she was. Mrs. Grassley might have, too, for that matter. Both have motive. Means is more iffy, especially for Mrs. Grassley. She's rather frail. Seventy-five, I think. The good doctor is around seventy. Not frail, but not Hercules either. Has something of a temper and cruel streak. Supposedly Mister and Missus were home together when Deloris and Jazmin were murdered."

Prudy walked into the office, jumped up on to Tina's desk and stretched out. Isis followed her and jumped onto Bea's lap. Manley jumped up onto the couch and curled up in the unoccupied corner.

Cal said, talking to the cats, "I'm not repeating any of this for you. You should have been here."

Tina smiled. Bea giggled. I took it for what it was. Cal stroking Tina.

"Harry, what's the address of the outfit you bought those stilettos from?"

"Just a minute." I checked the company's website and gave Cal the address.

He made a phone call. "Hey, Nelson, did we ask this company to check its records to see if it sold any stilettos to Minnesota citizens?" He gave her the name and address. "We did? Okay. Any response? None? Okay. Thanks."

"Okay. Next is Ashley Morgan. She worked for Catchfire, left, took a big account with her, and started her own firm. According to John Goldman, one of Deloris's co-workers, rumor has it Deloris Anderson was trying to get the account back. I talked to the president of Catchfire and he confirmed Morgan left to avoid being fired. Motive number one. Motive number two, Morgan and Anderson had an affair and Anderson dumped her."

"Before or after she left Catchfire?" Tina asked.

"Before. Motive number three, I confirmed with Roland, Inc. that when their contract was up with Ashley and Morgan they were very much inclined to go with Deloris Anderson. In the words of the Roland CEO, 'Ms. Anderson is the best in the city. Wouldn't you want the best working for you?' I had to admit I would."

"Plenty of motive for Morgan. Opportunity?" Tina asked.

"Says she was in Duluth with friends. We're trying to sort out their stories looking for holes. As for means, yeah, she could probably do it.

"And that leaves John Goldman. He's something of a sour grape. Pisses and moans about everything. Life's done nothing but shit on him. Very resentful of Anderson's advance. He and she started at the same time and he's gone nowhere while Anderson's 'fucked her way to the top'. His words. He has no remorse over her death. Said it couldn't have happened to a more deserving person. He lives at the Grant Apartments along the Loring Greenway. Perfect for keeping an eye on her, since her route took her past there. Alibi is weak. Said he was just getting up. Lives alone."

"But his motive isn't overly strong," Tina said.

"No, it isn't," Cal admitted.

"I'd like to start by taking a look at the crime scene," Tina said.

Cal nodded. "Let's go then."

"You, too, Harry," Tina continued. "Bea, you'll hold down the fort?"

"Sure thing."

Tina, Cal, and I bundled up, got into Cal's car, and headed off for downtown. When we arrived near the scene, Cal put on the flashing lights and we got out to take a look. Fresh snowfall had covered the original scene. But we could still get an idea. Right alongside West River Road is an asphalt walking and bike lane, which splits at the Hennepin bridge. One path continues on alongside the road, following the river, and the other crosses the road, follows it until it turns southwest on the other side of the bridge.

"From the position of the bodies and tracks in the snow, we figure the murderer was waiting there." Cal pointed to a spot under the bridge. "Then rushed Deloris and Jazmin before they made the turn to cross the road and continue on the other side."

Tina nodded, taking in the scene, and checking sight lines. "Seems to me," she said, "if the murderer was waiting there, where you said, Cal, he or she would have been easily seen once he or she started moving."

"That's how we figure it too. And the prints in the snow seem to indicate that's how it played out. These pepper spray guns have a range of twenty to twenty-five feet. If Deloris and Jazmin had relaxed their vigilance, it's possible the murderer could have gotten within range before they decided they needed to act. And then it was too late."

"Where was the witness?" I asked.

Cal said, "He was jogging behind the victims, saw the attack, and tried to help, when he got sprayed."

Tina thought a moment. "So all of this kind of rests on Jazmin getting lax. But what if Jazmin was in on it and the murderer took her out to silence her?"

Cal thought quite awhile on Tina's hypothesis and finally admitted he couldn't prove it wasn't that way. "But then the murderer and Jazmin had to have had a connection," he said.

Tina replied, "So? Who says they didn't?"

"God damn it, Wright. Isn't that making things a bit complex?"

Tina shrugged. "Who says it isn't?"

"You CIA types." Cal shook his head.

"What's the Company have to do with it?" she replied. "It's a possibility. Is it not?"

"It is."

"Then, it seems to me, it's a line of inquiry that should be pursued."

"Not everything is a conspiracy."

"No. But a Benjamin says one of our suspects knew Jazmin."

"You're on, Wright."

Tina looked at me and smiled. I smiled back. Even if she lost, she'd just gotten Cal to pursue a line of investigation he wasn't inclined to. These two really need to quit the folderol and at least admit they're a committed couple, or actually go get married. Then again it is pretty comical to watch them just as they are.

Cal was on the phone. "Nelson. Find out which of our suspects might have known Jazmin Washington." There was a pause. "Yeah. Well, this isn't vice. You're in the big leagues now." Another pause. "Get on it and let me know ASAP." He hung up.

I said, "Your new partner was in vice?"

"Yeah. Why?" Cal replied.

"Because Harry thinks she should be in a magazine," Tina said.

Cal burst out laughing. "Hear tell, she tricked potential johns undercover. A magazine might be too tame."

Snow was falling now and gusts of wind set it to swirling under the bridge and in the corners of buildings.

"Let's get out of the cold and get something to eat," Tina said.

"Good idea," Cal replied.

We got into the car and Cal drove over to the Northstar building, where we got malts and hot dogs, for Bea, as well, and headed back to Tina's place. By then the snow was coming down like crazy and the wind was blowing just under hurricane strength. The white stuff was driven with such intensity, needles out of a shotgun would have been welcome.

"I'm dropping you off," Cal said, "gotta run downtown and make sure Nelson is doing it right. I'll be back later." He gave Tina a kiss and me a salute and was off.

Tina and I went inside. I gave Bea her hot dog and malt.

"Thanks, Harry! Come here." I did and she gave me a kiss. "I love you. You always think of me."

I kissed her back. "Ditto."

"Any luck figuring stuff out?" Bea asked.

"Not sure," I said.

Tina went on into the office.

"But Tina came up with a line of investigation Cal hadn't thought of."

"Really? Wow." Bea took a bite of hot dog. "This is good," she said. At least that's what I think she said. Kind of difficult to understand someone who's mouth is full of hot dog.

I touched Bea's hair and smiled at her. She probably smiled back. But mouth full of hot dog, well... I went into the office.

"Do you really think Jazmin was in on it?"

Tina puffed on her cigar and took a drink of madeira. "Seems odd to me. She should have been more on guard than she appears to have been. That's all. From the reports she sent in everything was quiet from day one." She paused. "Let me check Jazmin's reports with Logan's." Tina brought up the reports on her computer and began going through them.

Five minutes became ten became twenty, I went out to Bea's desk and asked about supper.

"We have lots of leftovers, Harry, I thought we could just make our own suppers."

"Fine with me. The princess in there might be upset no one is making her something, but that's okay."

"Harry, you shouldn't talk about your sister that way."

"Harry!"

"Ah, the princess calleth," I said.

"Harry, you are wicked," Bea said.

"I am," I replied, and went to see what Tina had found.

"Look at this," she commanded.

I looked at the side by side reports and read the summary of Logan's watch and of Jazmin's. They were from consecutive days and not the same day, because they alternated duty days.

"What do you see?" Tina asked.

"Well, they both tell us there was nothing untoward happening on either day."

"Yes. What else?"

"Logan seems to have a better eye for detail. Jazmin seems to almost whitewash the events. Like airbrushing a photo."

"My impression exactly. In each report, Logan gave us a more detailed picture. Jazmin's were airbrushed, as it were."

"Perhaps it's just her style. She wasn't a detail person or felt there was no need to report on details which in the end weren't important."

"Or she was leaving out a detail that was important — like that of the murderer planning how to pull it off."

I shrugged. "We can't prove it either way."

"Not at this point we can't."

"Have you talked with Melissa or her sisters?"

"No. Nothing was happening. Unfortunately, I didn't pay close enough attention. But now, in hindsight, perhaps we see here an inkling, a hint, of collusion. I'll have to talk to Melissa and see if this was normal for Jazmin."

I looked outside. "Darn near blizzard conditions out there."

Tina nodded. "It's getting late in the day anyway, I'll call her tomorrow."

"You could email her."

"Good idea." Tina began tapping away at the keyboard. A few minutes later, she reported the email sent. "What's for supper?" she asked.

"MYO," I replied.

She gave me a perturbed face.

"Make Your Own. Bea says we have tons of leftovers we need to eat."

"I don't know what I pay you two for. Your bad habits have rubbed off on her already."

"Huh. Maybe you need a domestic."

"My ass. I have you two."

"Fine. I'll make you a sandwich."

"I'll make my own."

"Jeez. Who made you an EAP?"

"What the hell is that?"

"English American Princess."

She just shook her head and left."

I went out to Bea. "Yep. Princess."

"Harry. Be nice."

"Come on. Let's eat."

We nuked plates of leftover food. Tina wasn't in the dining room. Found her in the living room sitting before the fire, drinking madeira, and eating a sandwich. We joined her.

"Are you happy, Mrs. Wright?" Tina asked.

"Oh, yes, very happy, Tina. I can't thank you enough."

"I'm glad I helped you two get together. If we'd waited for Harry—"

"Hey! What are you picking on me for?"

"Just giving you crap."

"Okay. Next time I'll make you a sandwich."

"See how that works, Bea?"

"I see, Tina. Thanks for the tip." Bea looked at Tina and gave her a knowing nod and Tina winked back.

"Seriously, though," Tina continued, "I'm glad you two are happy."

"Tina, ask Cal to marry you," Bea said. "Just get it out there."

"Actually Cal asked me to marry him while you two were gone and I said I'm not ready."

"What?" I couldn't believe what I'd just heard. "What are you waiting for, Sis?"

"I'm like you, big brother. I got burned and I'm still licking my wounds."

"Let me tell you something," I continued, "I was scared to commit again. But I'm glad I did. You love Cal. I think it will do you both good to commit to each other."

"I suppose you're right."

"Of course I'm right."

"And don't make a pun."

Bea started giggling. "I'm right, too."

Tina rolled her eyes. "I think I asked for this."

Bea set her plate down, got up, went to Tina and kissed her. "You did. And we love you for it." Bea returned to her seat. "You know, my brother has been there to protect me. But I can't say we're close like you two. You really take care of each other and I'm glad I'm a member of your family. I feel loved, cared for, protected, valued, appreciated. And let me tell you, it's the greatest feeling on earth."

"Thanks, Bea," Tina said.

Bea continued, "It would be nice if Cal was part of this. I like him. He's a great guy. You know, if you don't want him I'll be glad to take him. Estrogen is fine. But I can't seem to get enough testosterone."

Tina and I busted up laughing. Tina finally managed to get out, "Nope. He's all mine."

"Drat it all, anyway." Bea put on a pouty face.

Just then Cal came in. "It's not fit for man or beast or even you, Wright, out there."

"Oh, really?" Tina said. "You could have just said 'beast.'"

"Huh. I've never heard you complain about me being a beast in the sack."

"True. Well, don't stand there looking like an orphan. Get your ass over here and kiss me."

"With pleasure." He went to where she was sitting, but she stood and they almost gave Bea and I a free show. "How's that?"

"Pretty good, Swenson. Your nose is cold. Let me warm you up." They parked on one end of the sofa wrapped up in a lover's knot. They didn't stay that way for long, though, before they decided to head off to bed, leaving Bea and I by ourselves sitting before the fire while the snow fell outside.

VI – Saturday, 4 January

DETECTION IS SOLVING A puzzle, or at least that is how it's usually characterized. To my mind, it's more like watching a movie from the middle. You start finding things out, but you have no context in which to put the data. Sometimes one doesn't even know one has a piece of information until a relationship is seen with other pieces of information. Couple that with misinformation or withheld information (whether accidentally or purposefully) or outright lies and detection is often more art than science.

Tina has noted, the spy game is more about people management than anything else. There is the outright theft of information, but more often the agent is managing others who have decided or have been convinced or bribed to steal and pass on information. Frequently detection is also about managing the suspects until one of them trips up or decides to confess.

Most instances of murder involve people who know each other and are fairly easily solved. Occasionally a murderer has gone to great lengths to avoid being caught. And sometimes they are successful in evading discovery.

Cal wanted to talk about the case, but Tina doesn't like conversation of any sort at breakfast. And especially business conversation. So Cal waited. When breakfast was over, Tina, Cal, and I retired to the office while Bea cleaned up dishes.

"Nelson couldn't get any of our suspects to admit she or he knew Jazmin Washington," Cal said.

"I'm not surprised," Tina replied. "I think you need to go at it from the other end."

Cal nodded. "I suppose you're right."

"Dead men or women tell no tales and tell no lies."

"True enough, I suppose." Cal took out his phone and made a call. The conversation was short, "Nelson, I want you—" A brief pause. "You're stuck in a snow-drift?" Another pause. "God damn it, Nelson, don't you know how to drive?" He shook his head, took a couple of deep breaths, and then continued, "Alright. Let me know when you're available."

"Aren't you a little tough on her?" Tina said.

"No."

"You better hope she isn't your boss one day."

Swenson didn't verbalize, he let his face do the talking.

I looked out the window. Snow was falling again. The wind looked nasty, too, the way the trees were swaying and the snow swirling around. The weather forecast wasn't great either. A perfect weekend to stay indoors and yet I had a feeling we were going to end up galli-vanting all over the countryside. Maybe it was time to retire and live off of Bea's money. A beach on Samoa was looking pretty doggone good about now.

Prudy wandered in and took a spot on one of the chairs. Manley followed and jumped on Tina's desk and stretched out on her blotter. Tina picked him up and put him in her lap.

"Say, Cal?"

"Yeah, Harry?"

"What happened to Anderson's dog?"

"In the pound, I think. Why?"

"Just curious. Cute little fellow."

"I suppose. If you like those little dogs."

Tina had been checking her iPad. "Melissa hasn't answered my email," she said and picked up her desk phone phone and punched in some numbers. After a moment she said, "Hey there, Melissa, Tina Wright. Do you have time for a few questions about Jazmin Washington?" A pause. "Terrible. She have family?" Pause. "Uh-huh. Have an address or phone?" Another pause. "Thanks Melissa. Say, I was wondering about her reports to me. Quite sketchy. Was that the norm for her?" Silence on Tina's end, except for a couple "uh-huhs," then, "Super. Thanks for the info. Bye."

"And?" I said.

"Jazmin has a mother, sister, and a brother here. The rest of her family is in Chicago. As for her reports, Melissa will scan one and email it to me for comparison. Here, Sweet Cheeks, the addresses for her family in Minneapolis."

Cal got up and took the paper Tina had pushed to the edge of her desk. He then got on the phone and in a minute got hold of Sergeant Nelson and gave her the addresses. After his call ended, he said, "I'd better get down to headquarters. See you all later." He got up, went to Tina's desk, kissed her good-bye, and left.

Tina checked her email. "Ah, Melissa's on top of it now. I'm going to forward to you, Harry."

"Okay." In a moment the email was in my in basket and I was looking at Jazmin's report from another job.

"What do you think, Harry?"

"Off hand I'd say she's more detailed here than in the other reports she provided for us."

"My opinion, too. We'll see what Cal is able to dig up. I'm willing to wager Jazmin and the murderer were in cahoots. Somehow, somewhere they knew each other and Jazmin decided to aid and abet."

"Well that just sucks if that's the case."

"Doesn't it though?"

"I mean we helped send Deloris Anderson to her death."

Tina nodded. "Bites the big one, it does. Now I really feel obligated to catch the bastard." She took out a Muniemaker Long and lit it.

Bea poked her head in. "Hey, guys, we eating lunch anytime soon?"

Tina scowled. She never re-lights a cigar and having just lit one I can understand the scowl. "Didn't you just have breakfast?" she asked.

"That was how long ago?" Bea protested.

"Are you pregnant?" I asked.

Bea got this shocked and then thoughtful look on her face. "Oh, God, Harry, do you think? I mean, I've been eating like a pig."

I looked at Tina and she had the goddamnedest smirk on her face.

"What are you smirking for? You'll have to listen to the pitter-patter of little feet and squalling in the night."

"You two are a hoot. Bea, I don't think so. But maybe you want to get a test kit."

"I'm forty-eight. That's not a good age to have a baby."

"Well, Babe, if you're pregnant, you're pregnant," I said. "Hopefully the baby will be healthy and there won't be any complications."

"Do you mean that, Harry?"

"Yes."

She ran into the office, sat in my lap, and hugged and kissed me. "I'd love to have your baby."

"Well, maybe you want to check it out with the drug store test kit before we do anymore speculating."

Tina blew out a cloud of cigar smoke. "Then again maybe Harry just agrees with you."

"Oh, yeah, maybe that's it," Bea said. "I have love munchies."

Tina burst out laughing and I let out a guffaw.

"You never heard of love munchies?"

"Can't say I have," Tina said. "I have the opposite reaction when I fall in love."

"Really?" Bea said. "Yeah, I'm probably not pregnant. Just married and in love. So can we have lunch now?"

Tina was laughing so hard she couldn't talk. She just waved us away.

"Come on, Babe. That hand gesture means, 'You two go on. I'll catch up later.'"

Bea got off my lap, took my hand, and pulled me out of the office. Into the kitchen we went where we made sandwiches, which were ready by the time Tina joined us. We hauled our grub to the dining room. I opened a bottle of Missouri Riesling.

"This is a rare delight," I said.

Tina raised her eyebrows.

I continued, "Yeah, Missouri Riesling was thought to be an extinct grape variety. But an enterprising wine maker found a vine at Cornell University, took cuttings, and is now making this great wine again."

Bea looked thoughtful. "Maybe we should be eating something other than hot dog sandwiches."

Tina laughed. "If Mr. Wine Connoisseur thinks this rare wine goes with hot dog sandwiches, who are we to question?"

Bea tasted the wine. "Wow. This is good. I like this."

"Better than beer?" I asked.

"Maybe," she replied.

We settled in to eating our sandwiches and chips and drinking wine. The meal was progressing nicely, with occasional chit-chat, when the phone rang. Bea took the call.

"Wright Investigations," she said. Her end of the conversation was: "Yes, we do surveillance." A pause. "Possibly. You'd have to make an appointment and talk with Miss Wright." Pause. "Uh-huh." A somewhat lengthy pause. "Right. Yes, you'd have..." A micro pause. "Sure, Monday, the sixth at ten-thirty. See you then, Mrs. Baker."

"She wants us to tail a wayward spouse," Tina said.

"Yes," Bea replied.

"Ugh. I hate those cases almost as much as finding missing persons."

"Are they difficult?" Bea asked.

"No. Just potentially messy and violent," Tina said.

"Oh. I can see that. You find out your spouse or lover is cheating on you, it can be devastating. When I discovered Alicia was cheating on me, I was glad to tell you the truth. I hoped she'd leave me. But not everyone's like me."

After a few minutes, Bea said, "Harry, if you ever want to be with someone else will you talk to me about it? Maybe we can work something out. I mean, I'd not want to but I'd share you to not lose you."

"You'd what?" Tina was flabbergasted.

"I'd accept another woman if it meant Harry wouldn't leave me. It's not ideal, from my perspective, but if you really didn't want to leave me, Harry, just wanted some variety, I could live with it."

Tina shook her head. "I'd kill him."

"Bea," I said. "I'm not interested in anyone else. Can't imagine I would be. But if it happens, we'll talk."

"Thanks, Harry. I don't want to lose you and I want you to be happy."

Tina shook her head. "Bea, I don't know what I think about your generosity. I couldn't do it."

"Tina, if you and Cal have a great relationship and then one of you has an interest in someone else but you don't want a divorce what do you do? You and Cal love each other, yet this other person is so very interesting. Now you have to deny yourself. But if Harry finds an interesting person, maybe I'd find her interesting too. If Harry is committed to me, why push him away because he's emotionally involved with me and someone else? Just a lot of loss. I'm tired of losing. Done it all my life."

"Babe, as far as I'm concerned," I said, "this is all academic. But thank you for sharing your thoughts."

Tina said, "Don't you want Harry all to yourself?"

"Sure I do," Bea replied, "But I'd rather let him play with the neighbor girl than lose him altogether."

Tina just grunted. I said, "There are more and more studies coming out which suggest a little infidelity or time off from the spouse might be good for a long-term relationship. You and Cal practice taking time off but you always come back to each other."

Tina was thoughtful and finally said, "We do. I guess I want to be with him more than anyone else."

"That's what I'm saying." Bea was triumphant.

"I guess I get it," Tina said. She drank wine. "This really is very good. Missouri Riesling. Hope they make more."

We finished our lunch and returned to work. Tina going over information Cal had gathered on Deloris Anderson's death and that of Jazmin Washington. I checked out our potential client, Tremonisha Baker.

And Bea busied herself with supper preparations, while keeping an eye on the phone.

Cal showed up a little before five. "God it's cold out there. Eleven above, five below wind chill, and a wind that will strip bark off trees."

"Want something to drink?" Tina asked.

"You don't have coffee. That's what I'd really like. A hot cup of coffee."

"Sorry. Tea is it. You know I hate coffee and won't have the stench of it in my house."

Cal shook his head. "I guess beggars can't be choosers," he said.

I went out to the kitchen to get Cal a cup of tea. When I came back, he and Tina were talking about the case. Cal was speaking.

"And finally hit the jackpot. Jazmin and her siblings went to Edina High School, where Ashley Morgan also went."

Tina replied, "So, at least in theory, they could know each other."

"In theory, yes."

I gave Cal his cup of tea. He told me thanks. I sat at my desk.

Cal continued. "Now we need to establish if there was a connection to give credence to your theory."

"Morgan have siblings?" Tina asked.

"A brother. Two years older." Cal drank tea.

"He went to Edina?"

Cal nodded.

"Did you take a look at the school yearbooks?" Tina asked.

"Not yet."

"There's a connection somewhere," Tina said.

"That's what you keep saying." Cal finished his tea and got up. "We eating anytime soon?"

Tina smiled. "I guess we have two who are pregnant."

"What?" Cal said.

"You had to have been here earlier," I answered and went on to explain about the earlier conversation. Cal started laughing and Bea poked her head in letting us know she heard us making fun of her.

"It's only because we love you, Bea," Tina said.

"Well, FYI, supper in ten," Bea said.

"Come on, Bea." Cal put his arm around her. "Let's leave these hoity-toits to their own devices."

"It's a deal." Bea laughed as she and Cal left.

"I hope this lasts, Harry." Tina said.

"What lasts?"

"This great big happy."

"Yeah. Sure would be nice."

VII – Monday, 6 January

SUNDAY WAS BITTERLY COLD. The temp didn't get above zero and we had more snowfall in the evening. Not a lot, but at this point any amount was too much. We stayed home, all four of us, and played a many hours long marathon game of Monopoly. By the way, I hate Monopoly. But to please Bea, I played. The things you do for love.

This morning Bea and I made breakfast. Pancakes. Buckwheat pancakes. The wind chill was forty-five below and I felt like something hearty to start the day. After breakfast, Cal took off for downtown and Tina went to the office. Bea and I cleaned up the kitchen and joined Tina to wait for our potential client.

Tremonisha Baker was a half-hour late for her appointment and blamed the weather. A convenient scapegoat. She and Tina talked for half an hour. The request was simple: catch her husband in the act of screwing his girlfriend so Mrs. Baker could strip him of every last dime when she filed for divorce.

However, I could tell Tina wasn't interested in the case. She suggested marriage counseling and Mrs. Baker wasn't interested. She wanted to humiliate his wallet for his humiliation of her. So Tina said she'd need a five thousand dollar retainer and, because she'd have to have the services of several detectives to be successful at the surveillance, the cost would be five hundred dollars per hour. Mrs. Baker balked, tried to negotiate, and eventually said, "Thanks, but no thanks."

When our non-client had departed, Tina lit a cigar and poured herself a glass of madeira.

"Five hundred an hour. Seriously?" I said.

"My rate, your rate, and the rates of one or two extras. This is a business. Not an altruistic do-good society. Besides. I'm the best. I must charge accordingly."

"Good grief."

The phone rang and Bea routed it through to Tina. She listened and a big smile broke out on her face. "Thanks, Sweet Cheeks," she said at last and hung up the phone. "Jazmin was a cheerleader when Ashley's brother was on the football team."

"Potential connection," I replied.

"Yes, indeed." She thought a minute, then said, "We need to talk to Ashley Morgan's brother." She picked up the phone, punched in numbers, and waited.

"Hey, Sweet Cheeks, we need to talk to Ashley's brother." There was a pause, and then, "Sweet. See you later."

"Cal already working on it?" I said.

"Yep. I'm rubbing off on him."

I shook my head.

"He'll be by later to pick us up," Tina added.

"Great. We get to go along." I got up and went out to Bea's desk to let her know the plan.

▼

A couple hours later we were in James Bradford Morgan's office. He informed us to call him 'Jim'.

"What can I do for you?" he asked.

Jim still looked every bit the football player. He'd taken care of himself and hadn't run to fat. He still had the jock mentality and was sizing up both Tina and Nikki, which is what I heard Cal call Sergeant Nelson when he wasn't calling her 'Nelson'. And he himself was making sure there wasn't a molecule of something out of place and that they had his best profile. Tina ignored him, but I could see Sergeant Nelson stepping to the dance.

Tina asked, in answer to Jim's question, "Did you know Jazmin Washington?"

"Not recently."

"How well did you know her in high school?"

He smiled. "Jazmin was a cheerleader and made herself very popular with the guys on the team."

Tina continued, "Any rumors about her being gay?"

"Not that I recall. If she was into women, that must've come later."

"Did your sister know Jazmin?"

"In high school? Possibly. I didn't pay much attention to my sister's friends."

"What about now?"

"Still don't. We aren't all that close."

"Would you say your sister's a lesbian?"

"I don't see—"

"Just answer the question," Cal said.

"It was a fad of hers for awhile," Jim Morgan answered.

"When was this?" Tina asked.

"Oh, I don't know. Maybe a couple years after college?"

"But not now," Tina pressed.

"Look, I don't know who or what she's having sex with. You're going to have to ask her."

"You ever bring Jazmin home when you were in high school?"

"Are you kidding? She wasn't anywhere near our social standing. My parents would have killed me. Jazmin was the kind of girl you met at parties or took someplace. You didn't go out on a date with her."

"I see," Tina replied. "I think I'm done."

We left and made our way to Cal's Ford and piled in. "God, is he a pig or what?" Nikki said.

Tina said, "I wouldn't insult pigs. They're better than he."

"You got that right," Nikki replied.

"Cal, do we have a picture of Jazmin? Recent?" Tina asked.

"Not sure. If we don't, I can probably get one."

"And Ashley Morgan?"

"Same. Why? You want to shop them around?"

"I do. I have a hunch."

"Do tell," he replied.

"I think Jazmin and Ashley were seeing each other fairly recently."

"Okay. I'll see what we can come up with."

"Would you email the pics when you get them?"

"Sure."

Cal dropped Tina and me off at home and then drove on to downtown.

"So what do you make of what Jim had to say?" I asked once we were inside.

"Seems to me that, aside from being a disgusting example of the worst of the male sex, he was probably on the up and up."

"So you want to show the pics around?"

"I do. I'll be doin' the queer girl scene."

We had walked into the kitchen when Tina made that comment.

"What did you say?" Bea was looking at us and I couldn't tell if she was getting ready for a fight or just didn't hear us.

"I'm going to show some pics around the lesbian bars," Tina said.

Bea laughed. "They're going to know you're straight, you know."

"Okay," Tina replied.

"They might not open up about the sisters to you."

"Hmm. Don't think I can pull it off?"

Bea looked at her. "Hmm. Come here." Tina stood next to her. "Bend down a little." Tina did. Bea then put her arms around Tina's neck and kissed her full on the mouth. But when Bea gave her some tongue, Tina pulled back in a hurry.

"Holy shit, Bea. I didn't expect that."

Bea was doubled up with laughter and couldn't talk. I too was laughing.

"Alright," Tina said. "Have a laugh at my expense."

When Bea finally had herself under control, she said, "You might pass for being fresh out of the closet, but that's a pretty iffy 'might'. Why don't I do it? Might even meet people I know. I think I'll get a better response."

"If you want to," Tina said.

"Sure. Not a problem."

Tina shook her head. "All I have to say is you're a damn good kisser, Bea. Got me all wet."

Bea and I had laughter melt down. Couldn't breathe, let alone talk.

"Alright, you two,"

And because we were still laughing, Tina just shook her head and walked out of the kitchen.

▼

Cal showed up a little after eight.

"Cal," I began, "I just want you to know I'm doing my best to keep Bea satisfied. But she might have unleashed Tina's inner gay."

He looked at me. "What the hell are you talking about, Major?"

"Well, maybe you best talk to Tina."

Tina explained about the afternoon.

"Oh, yeah. I forgot you were with the Harris woman," Cal said. Then he looked from Bea to Tina and back to Bea and then back to Tina. "Really?"

Tina nodded. "What I can't figure out is why Harry dragged his feet on getting married. Shit. If you kissed like that, Swenson, I'd have said yes years ago."

Cal looked at Bea, looked at me, shook his head, and went out to the kitchen. He came back with a beer.

After taking a pull on the bottle, he said, "I have the photos so anytime Juliet here wants to go to work she can." He took another pull. "You know, this house is a wee bit strange."

All three of us busted up laughing, leaving Cal to shake his head and drink beer.

VIII - Saturday, 11 January

BEA HIT THE JACKPOT last night. All week nothing, but last night she got confirmation from three women they'd seen Ashley and Jazmin together at a couple of different bars on several occasions. Tina was ecstatic and Cal said the information might provide us with what we needed to crack the case wide open.

"Looks to me Morgan was lying," he said. "She not only knew Jazmin, it seems clear there was something going on between them."

"Thank you very much, Bea, for doing this," Tina said.

"I'm glad I could help," she replied. "It helped me too."

"How so?" I asked.

"I know I like men and one man in particular," she replied and gave me a kiss.

"Thanks, Babe. I'm glad you do. You are the best thing to happen to me."

To me, she said, "And you to me. I love you, Harry." To Cal, she asked, "So now what happens?"

He said, "We start questioning Morgan and checking into her movements. Hopefully we can break her sooner rather than later. A search warrant isn't out of the question either."

"I assume you're watching her movements," Tina said.

"Have two women and a man on her since last night when Bea broke the news. I'd like to search her place, but I seriously doubt she still has the weapon or clothes. Unless she isn't very bright, which I doubt."

"If I wasn't working for you, I could do it," Tina said.

"And have you get your ass in jail for breaking and entering? No thanks."

"How sweet of you to care, Cal. I'm touched."

He just rolled his eyes.

"Let's talk to her today," Tina said.

"I'm all for it," Cal replied. He made a phone call and, when he was done, said she was still at home. He looked at his watch and announced the time was ten thirty-eight.

We left Bea to hold down the fort and the three of us drove across town to Ashley Morgan's place. Cal knocked on the door and rang the doorbell. When she realized who was at her door, she reluctantly let us enter and led us to what I took to be a living room.

"Have a seat," she said. "Please excuse my appearance, but it is on the early side of the day."

Cal spoke, "Sorry, but murder is messy and it inconveniences everyone even remotely connected. Miss Wright and her brother are consultants to the department and she'd like to ask a few questions to help clear up some issues."

"I already gave a statement and I've already been questioned."

"It's like a game of Clue," I said. "You keep asking questions until the pieces finally fall into place. Sometimes the other players don't give you what you're looking for — at least willingly until you force them to."

Ashley nodded her blond head.

Tina began, "You denied knowing Jazmin Washington. Why?"

"Why not? My personal life is my business."

"Not when it comes to a murder investigation, Ms. Morgan."

"Well, now you know."

"How did you know we knew?"

"Someone told me Alicia Harris's wife was asking about Jazmin and me. Thought I ought to know."

Tina nodded, thought for a moment, then asked, "Were you and Jazmin intimate in high school?"

"No. I knew her, but not well."

"So when did you?"

"When did I what?"

"Become intimate?"

"Who says we were?"

"You were seen with her several times by at least three people. Were you or were you not intimate with her?"

"Yes, we were 'intimate'. As you put it."

"If you weren't close in high school, how did you get close now?"

"I knew her brother from one of my classes. Went out with him a few times. When Jazmin came back from the Marines, she looked me up. She was trying to find work."

There was a sneeze from another part of the condo.

"You have company?" Cal asked.

"Brent. We live together. He's my regular partner."

"Poly?" I said.

Ashley looked at me. Then said, "Yeah. Brent and I have been together eight years. But we occasionally get involved with others."

"I take it then," Tina said, "you were living with Brent when you were seeing Deloris Anderson?"

"Yes."

"Why didn't you tell us about him?" Cal asked.

"Why should I?"

"Like maybe an alibi," he replied.

"He was in Florida spending time with his girlfriend. He wasn't here. Why get him involved?"

"Well, he's involved now. Go get him."

"Never mind," a voice said, followed by the appearance of the person to whom the voice belonged. "I'm here."

Ashley said, "This is Brent Trenholm."

He nodded to us and we introduced ourselves.

Cal told him to have a seat. We'd get to him shortly.

Tina continued, "Tell me about Deloris Anderson."

"What's to tell? The bitch got me fired."

"According to your former boss you resigned."

"Yeah. Resign or be fired. So I resigned, took a juicy account with me, and started my own company."

"Deloris was trying to get the account back."

"Of course. She's a bitch or was, I should say. I'm so glad somebody offed her."

"When did you last see Anderson?" Tina asked.

"Look. It's very simple. The cunt and I had a brief fling. Meribeth spoiled it for me—"

"Wait," Cal said. "Who's Meribeth?"

"A friend. But she can be mean and she was with Deloris one night and Deloris cut everything off and then worked to get me fired. And to be even meaner, she was going to take my account away. I haven't seen her or talked to her since Catchfire."

Cal was puzzled. "Who can be mean?"

"Meribeth. BDSM and shit like that."

"And she's your friend?" Tina asked.

"Yeah." Ashley got very quiet.

We all sat there waiting. But Ashley said nothing. Brent, too, just sat there. Cal and I looked at Tina, who just sat there. We know her well enough to just let her sit if she chooses to. Finally she spoke.

"How often do you do things with Meribeth?"

"She's around," Ashley said. "Maybe once a week."

"Was she around when Brent was gone?"

"Yes, she was around."

"Did you do stuff with her?"

"Yes. She can be very pushy. Just kind of takes over, ya know?"

"I think I do," Tina said. "Did she 'take over' when Brent was gone?"

Brent intervened. "I think we're done here until we get a lawyer."

"And why would you need a lawyer?" Cal asked.

"I think you know why," he said. "Please leave."

Tina stood. Cal and I also stood. Tina said, "Either way, the future will be difficult."

We left and on the way to the car, Cal said, "What the hell does that comment mean?"

Tina said, "I believe Ashley may have dissociative identity disorder."

"Good God," Cal exclaimed.

"My guess is, 'Meribeth' committed the murder."

"I don't believe you're saying this."

"Brent must be a stabilizing influence. Along with perhaps meds for depression. When he's not around, she is probably more likely to need the other persona."

"On your side, Cal," I interjected, "did you see the wall display over the gas fireplace?"

"Yeah."

"Wherever Brent got those swords, I bet you'll find out they sold him or Ashley the stiletto."

"Thanks, Harry. That will help us narrow things. But you think she's nuts."

Tina shrugged. "I'm no shrink, Cal, but look at it. Ashley is not on the up and up. She hid she knew Jazmin. She hid Brent. She hid Meribeth. Meribeth might be a real person. But I'm guessing by Brent's reaction she isn't. Meribeth is an alter."

"I think it's hokum," Cal said.

"It might be. Many professionals don't accept DID as real. Many murderers have faked DID to try to get off the hook. But the human mind is a funny thing. Insanity exists. People develop unusual or bizarre constructs or behaviors to cope with a reality they find difficult or impossible to cope with. To my mind, I think DID is possible. I'm not sure it's all that prevalent, but I do think it exists. Diagnosis goes all the way back to Paracelsus in the seventeenth century."

Cal looked at her and said, "Where the hell do you come up with this shit?"

"I read, Sweet Cheeks. Maybe you ought to try it sometime."

Cal shook his head and we got into his car. He dropped us off at home and headed back downtown. In the office, Tina sat at her desk, lit a cigar, and poured herself a glass of madeira.

"Do you really believe this or are you BSing Cal?"

"About Ashley having DID?"

I nodded.

"I have a hunch."

"I see."

"We need more evidence. But Brent clamoring for a lawyer indicates to me something is going on."

"It did seem awfully sudden. And I bet he got those swords from the same place I got my stilettos."

Tina puffed on her cigar and drank madeira and stared off into space. After a time she asked, "Can you get Gwen Poisson on the phone?"

"Sure." I dialed her number. After four rings she answered. "Hey Gwen, Harry Wright here." She greeted me and I told her, Tina had a question for her.

Tina got on the line and I stayed on. "Hi, Gwen."

"Hey, Tina."

"What I want you to do is hack into a company's file of mail order clients and find out if they shipped something to one of our suspects. Are you willing to do that?"

"You haven't asked me to do cyber-snooping for a long time. Sure. I can give it a shot."

"Thanks, Gwen. Harry will give you the details."

Which I did. Gwen said she'd get back to us as soon as she could.

"So now what?" I asked Tina.

"We wait," she replied and looked at the clock on her desk. "Isn't it about time for Bea to eat? Gotta keep the new mother well fed."

"Very funny."

Bea poked her head into the office. "You guys interested in gyros for supper?"

Tina started laughing and snorted the madeira she'd sipped. I simply shook my head and grinned.

"What?" Bea said.

"Tina said it was your feeding time," I told her.

She giggled. "I'm like clockwork. So. You ready to go?"

Tina recovered and indicated we were ready.

IX - Sunday, 12 January

CAL CAME HOME EARLY in the morning, about three or a little before. He'd gotten a search warrant and searched Ashley's home looking for the stiletto and the black jogging suit the witness had said the attacker was wearing. He came up empty handed and was in a pretty foul mood. He was still in a foul humor when he came down for breakfast. With Tina and Cal not saying anything, the atmosphere around the breakfast table was pretty quiet. When we were done eating, Cal called Nelson and asked how she was coming on verifying the Duluth alibis for Ashley. From his response, I took it she was working on it.

He sat in the living room and laid out game after game of Klondike solitaire on the coffee table. Tina set up an easel and began painting. Bea was tatting and I was figuring out a chess move. We were clearly hung up. We pretty much knew who the culprit was, but couldn't nail down how the deed was done. Everything seemed to hinge on one of the Duluth party cracking. We were also missing the weapon and the suspected seller wasn't cooperating in divulging whether or not our suspects had purchased a stiletto from them. Frustration all around.

And so, on a late Sunday morning in mid-January, we sat in the living room doing anything but detecting.

At twelve-thirty, Bea reminded us it was lunchtime. In a fit of frustration, Cal swept the cards off the table. "Can't even win at a goddamn game of cards." He scooped up the cards from the floor, put them back in the box and announced he was going downtown. He kissed Tina goodbye and left.

Bea waited a bit and said, "It's still lunchtime, guys. Is it MYO?"

I said, "Cal's gone and Tina's in the middle of painting. I think we're on our own."

"You want me to make you something?"

"Come on."

"Where we going?"

"Tavern on Grand."

"I'll drive."

We got into Bea's bright yellow Fiat and took off for St. Paul. The temperature was a balmy thirty-nine and even the wind chill was above freezing. When the temp is like this in January in Minnesota, everyone and God is out and today was no exception.

Even with Bea's tiny Fiat, we couldn't find a place to park within four blocks of the tavern and when we finally found a spot, we had to contend with a packed restaurant. We waited over forty-five minutes for a table and finally got lucky, ending up with a booth.

After much hemming and hawing, I ordered a bowl of chicken and wild rice soup and a bowl of chili. Bea got the walleye basket. Since she was driving she ordered a root beer and I decided on a Summit Pale Ale.

"You know, Harry, those girls aren't going to give anything away."

"Why not?"

"They're protecting a sister. It's like family. You see, you're a minority. The majority despises you. So you stick together, you protect your own."

"Wasn't Deloris a sister?"

"No. She was just using people. She wasn't gay. Just like I guess I'm not either."

"But you think Ashley is?"

"Well, I'm thinking maybe Ashley isn't but maybe this Meribeth is."

"Hm. It's a thought," I said. "But regardless if the person is called Ashley or Meribeth or both, the Duluth party isn't going to fink on her."

"I don't think so. Unless somebody is able to trip them up."

"And so far, no dice."

"But maybe Ashley didn't do it."

"Possible. But who?"

"I don't know."

"That's the problem. She or her brother have the strongest motives."

Our food came and we set to eating.

If Bea's right, then we will probably not break the alibis of Ashley's friends unless they are grilled separately. Which, I'm sure Cal's people are doing. It's SOP. So if they're hanging together, then they had to have rehearsed the story. And rehearsed it well. Which means they are all aiding and abetting.

So what's in it for them, other than loyalty to another member of your minority group? Maybe that's sufficient, but I find that idea a little hard to swallow. Maybe they all work for Ashley and Morgan. If they do, the police already know that. Could they have all been involved? A murder on the Orient Express set up? Hmm. We were at the scene. Of course weather had obliterated the original scene. The police should have taken photos, though.

I took out my cell and rang Tina. "Yes, Harry?"

"Say, Gwen needs to check if a stiletto was bought by one of Ashley's friends who was up in Duluth."

"Right. Thanks." She disconnected.

Bea asked, "You have an idea? I was wondering why you were so quiet."

"You ever read Murder on the Orient Express?"

"No. To be honest I don't like mysteries."

I laughed. "Now that is what I call ironic."

Bea giggled. "I guess so."

"Basically, a group of people on a train murder one of the other passengers. That's the story. What I'm wondering is if we have the same situation here."

"I see. You're thinking Ashley and her friends killed Deloris and Jazmin."

"Something like that. They were all involved in some way."

"Wow. That's different."

"When we get home I'll bounce it off Tina. Personally, I think it has merit."

"I do too. You're good, Harry."

"Not really, but thanks for the vote of confidence."

We finished eating. For Tina, I ordered a walleye sandwich with fries to go. Not sure she'd want it, but if she did she had it.

I paid for everything and we left. On the way to Bea's car we held hands. To be honest, at that moment, I didn't care if we solved anything. In the very core of my being I was happy. Not just content, but ecstatically happy. I was brimming over with joy. We reached the car, got in, and drove on home.

Tina was still working on her painting when we came in from outside.

"Brought you a walleye sandwich and fries from Tavern on Grand, if you're interested," I told her.

"Okay. Thanks."

"Want it now?"

"Uh, sure. In a minute."

"Okay. I'll heat up the fries for you."

"Thanks."

When I'd heated up the fries I called Tina to come and get it.

"So what's with your call earlier?" she asked.

"I'm thinking Ashley and her friends were all in on it."

"Possibly." She ate French fries.

Bea added, "Harry's theory might explain why the police can't find contradictions in their alibis."

"True." Tina ate more fries.

"Do you think my idea has merit?"

"It's a possibility, Harry." She put a fry in her mouth, chewed, swallowed, and asked, "You been reading Christie again?"

"Well, why not?"

"How long have we been working together?"

"I don't know. What five, six years?"

"Long enough for you to know detective work is dull, boring routine. Most crimes aren't spectacular and it's the plodding and monotonous routine that solves them. You also know, PIs rarely, if ever, get to work on murder cases. Fiction aside, real world gumshoes are kind of like insurance agents. If mystery writers wrote about real PIs, they wouldn't sell a goddamn book. Instead they have to invent these cute little bullshit puzzles for their PI to solve and titillate the reader. Mystery fiction is pure fantasy."

"But you're working on a murder," Bea said.

"Only because I know Cal and someone in the department was impressed I was in the CIA. Otherwise, I wouldn't get closer to a murder than the evening news."

"Oh," Bea replied.

"So you don't like my idea," I said.

"Actually, it may have merit. I'll have to think about it." She put French fries in her mouth.

▼

Cal showed up at suppertime. His mood hadn't improved much. He did join us to get a share of the vegan vegetable soup and tostadas I'd made. Halfway through the meal the phone rang. I saw it was Gwen and figured it was important.

"Hey Gwen!" I said.

"Hey. Tell Tina I've emailed her the information."

"Thanks Gwen. Let me know how many hours and I'll send a check."

"Thanks, Harry."

We ended the call. To Tina, I said, "You have a present in your email."

"Good," she replied.

Cal, with a spoon of soup halfway to his mouth, asked, "Do I want to know what Gwen was getting for you?"

"Maybe," Tina replied. "Just don't ask how."

He rolled his eyes and shook his head, then decided he wanted the spoonful of soup and let it finish its journey to its intended destination.

Bea's face was all puzzlement. "Did Gwen do something illegal? I'm confused."

Cal spoke. "Probably. And the Red Baron here is trying to spare me."

"Oh, I see."

Cal continued, "So what the hell was Gwen doing?"

"Research," Tina said.

"Okay. What did she find?"

"Don't know. Just a sec." Tina left the table and came back with her iPad. She tapped on it and then a great big smile broke out on her face. "Here Sweet Cheeks." She handed him the tablet.

"Oh, this is sweet," he said. He sat back and it was obvious the little grey cells were hard at work. Then he got his phone and told it to call Nelson. He then said, "Nelson. You need to get us a search warrant. Pronto." He gave her name, address, what they were looking for, where they expected it to be, and who'd be doing the search. "Get on it and I'm coming in."

He ate another spoon of soup, wolfed down a tostada, kissed Tina, and said he had to run. Halfway out of the dining room he turned and said, "Great supper, Major. Sorry I had to eat and run."

"No problem," I replied. "Catch some bad guys."

He gave me a salute and was off.

Tina sat back in her chair. "She's not going to have it and where she lives she could have gotten rid of it anywhere. But I have an idea."

And seeing that smile on Tina's face. I knew it was a doozy.

X – Monday, 13 January

TINA WAS RIGHT. CAL came up empty handed again. And he was pissed. So pissed, in fact, he didn't show up until after breakfast. Tina and I were in the office and Bea at her desk, when Cal came in and threw himself down on the couch.

"You aren't even going to give me a kiss?" Tina said.

He got up, went to her, bent down, and kissed her.

"Thank you," Tina said and added, "I love you, Cal Swenson."

He took her hand and pulled her to her feet. His arms went around her and hers around him and they shared one hell of a kiss. When they came up for air, he said, "I love you, Tina Wright."

Her voice quite soft, she said, "Thank you for loving me, Cal." Kissed him once again and then said, "Can you get them all here?"

"What?"

"The group. Ashley, her friends who went to Duluth with her, Brent. Can you get them here? We're going to try to bust this thing open."

"What do you know that I don't know?"

"Nothing. But Harry has a stiletto just like the one that was used to kill Deloris and Jazmin and we are going to see how good our bluffing game is."

"I'm in. I'll see what I can do." Cal then called Nelson and told her to round everyone up and get them to Tina's place ASAP. He looked at me, "Any breakfast leftovers, Major?"

"Sure. What would our man in blue like?"

"Surprise me."

"Gotcha." I left and went to the kitchen. I rustled up some eggs, sausage, and toast for our boy and took the plate to the office for him.

"Thanks, Harry." To Tina, he said, "You really think you can pull this off?"

She shrugged. "I think I have a seventy-five, maybe even eighty percent chance of doing so."

"Okay. I'll run with it. You can't bat any worse than what I've been doing."

We spent the next hour planning how the meeting would go to the best of our ability to predict the future. In the end, Tina either broke them down with her bluff or she didn't and we were left still trying to get on base.

▼

Sergeant Nelson finally called at three to let us know they all promised to be at Tina's place at eight. According to Cal, Nelson told them if they weren't there a squad would be around to pick them up.

Bea and I worked on refreshments and Cal and Tina worked out the seating. For beverages, I planned on hot tea, red and white wine, a selection of mixers, Scotch, gin, bourbon, dark and light rum, vodka, and beer. Bea and I made canapés: pickled herring on potato slices with beets and scallions; cheese and salami, with red bell pepper, sweet mustard, and cocktail onions on rye bread; and Radish Canapés Leeds.

For supper, Bea ran out and picked up chicken from the Colonel. We ate, cleaned up the dishes, and then waited for our guests to arrive. Tina doesn't do a show very often, but when she does it means her confidence level is very high.

The first to arrive was Sergeant Nikki Nelson. Close on her heels were our first guests, Kelly Cook and Robyn Guy. Secretary and Office Manager, respectively. Nikki made introductions and I invited our guests to partake of a beverage and canapés. Kelly made a Vodka Seven and Robyn, a Rum and Coke. Not long after, Linda Williams rang our doorbell. Bea got her name, let her in, and introduced her to me. Linda informed me she is the sales manager for Ashley and Morgan. I invited her to partake of a beverage and canapés. She poured herself a glass of white wine, took two Radish Canapés Leeds and one of the cheese and salami, and sat in her designated seat.

We had about a seven minute wait, when, precisely at eight o'clock, Stephanie LeGrande arrived. A designer for Ashley and Morgan, she looked like an advert for Ralph Lauren. She too chose white wine and took three Radish Canapés Leeds. I guided her from where she wanted to sit to where we wanted her to sit. She pouted.

The four women said little. They ate and drank. Every now and then Robyn and Kelly exchanged hushed words, which was easy for them because they were sitting together. They were positioned on stage left. Kelly on the end and then Robyn. On the other end of the row, sat Stephanie and seated in from stage right was Linda. The center chairs were for Ashley, on stage left side, and Brent on the stage right side.

Kelly and Robyn nursed their drinks, Linda maybe took one sip of her wine, Stephanie downed hers and got a refill. When the clock informed us the time was quarter after eight, Nelson stepped out to our waiting area and made a phone call. She came back a moment later and said Ashley and Brent were on their way. Another ten minutes passed before they were present and accounted for. Brent Trenholm, true to his Scandinavian heritage, loaded up on the pickled herring canapés and took a beer. Ashley poured herself a lemon sour, put a maraschino cherry in the glass and sat in her appointed chair.

When everyone was comfy, I gave Bea the signal and in a moment in walked the indomitable Justinia Wright. She was wearing a black pinstripe skirt suit. Her white blouse was adorned with a necklace of flat red stones. Her god-given six-foot stature was augmented by three-inch black stiletto high heels and her fiery red hair in a bun on top of her head. In her black suit, she dominated the room.

She stood to the side of her desk and said, "Thank you for coming. For those of you who don't know me, I am Justinia Wright. I have been, at the police department's request, assisting them in solving the murder of my client Deloris Anderson and her bodyguard, Jazmin Washington. My hope is that you will help me bring this investigation to a close tonight. Any questions?"

"Yes," Brent said. "Why am I here?"

"You live with Ashley Morgan," Tina replied.

He shrugged and drank beer.

Tina then asked those she didn't know to introduce themselves. Introductions over, she sat at her desk. "Perhaps the best procedure is for me to outline what happened. You may correct me if I error."

"How do you know what happened?" Stephanie asked while getting up for her third glass of wine. Brent joined her and got another beer.

"I've been at this for a long time," Tina replied.

"Only seven years," Brent replied.

Tina smiled. "As a private detective. Before this I worked for the CIA."

Stephanie formed an "O" with her mouth and drank wine.

Brent took a swig of beer from the bottle, then said, "Let's get this farce going. I have things to do."

"So do we all, Mr. Trenholm," Tina said. "Deloris Anderson, by all accounts, was not a pleasant person."

Ashley suddenly said, "What happened to her dog?"

Tina looked at Cal. He said the dog had been taken to a shelter.

Ashley nodded and said, "It suddenly dawned on me she had that little dog and I hoped someone gave it a good home."

Brent drank beer and said, "Shelter's probably better for the animal than being with that bitch Anderson."

Tina jumped on Trenholm's comment. "Yes, apparently Ms. Anderson was not a pleasant person. You, Miss Morgan, suffered at her hands."

Ashley nodded.

"She jilts you, then forces you to leave your job, and then proceeds to take away your most lucrative client."

Ashley nodded.

"Plenty of cause to want her dead. Wouldn't you say?"

Ashley nodded again.

"And with your partner's penchant for sharp instruments of death, you had the means available to do her in."

Ashley nodded again.

"But the cops didn't find anything, did they?" Brent said. His tone at once nasty and triumphant.

"No they didn't. Nor did they when they searched your home, Miss Cook."

"No, they didn't. Made quite a mess that I had to clean up."

I saw Nikki, standing at the back of the room, smile slightly. Cal, sitting on the couch behind our sextet, had no reaction. Routine is routine.

"Christmas week, Mr. Trenholm went out of town and the rest of you went to Duluth."

Heads nodded.

"However, on Christmas Day, you five drove back to the cities and early the next morning brutally and savagely murdered Deloris Anderson and Jazmin Washington. You all then drove back up to Duluth and returned, as planned, on Saturday."

Kelly Cook was staring daggers at Tina. Stephanie got up for another glass of wine. Linda Williams, Robyn Guy, and Ashley Morgan were shaking their heads.

"Miss Williams, Miss Guy, Miss Morgan you are shaking your heads. I'm not correct?"

Kelly Cook spoke, "You know you're fishing. We were in Duluth and you can't prove otherwise."

"We didn't have the opportunity. We weren't here," Robyn said.

"And there's no weapon," Linda Williams said. "Where's the weapon?"

Tina nodded. "Yes, that is a problem. But it's not unsolvable. When you all found out Deloris Anderson would probably take Roland, Inc. back into the Catchfire fold, I suppose you, Miss Guy, being the office manager, realized Ashley and Morgan would be in a world of hurt. Perhaps not even survive. So you or Miss Cook, which one?"

They sat as though they had become mannequins.

"Doesn't matter, really. One or both of you convinced the others Deloris Anderson had to go. A simple case of survival. It was a major boon for you Miss Morgan's friend, Jazmin Washington had been hired to be Miss Anderson's bodyguard. Because once you gained Miss Washington's confidence, your job became easier. Didn't it?"

No one said anything. Stephanie, however, did proceed to finish off the bottle of wine.

"The one issue, and this is where I'm guessing, is Miss Washington wasn't open to murder. So you had to murder her too."

Linda Williams stood up. "I'm leaving. I've had quite enough."

Cal said, "Sit down Ms. Williams. Unless all of you want to finish this downtown."

Linda hesitated and then said, "This is ridiculous. It's a nice story. But where's the proof?"

Tina continued, "The police are already working on finding someone who saw you in Minneapolis on Christmas Day or someone who saw you leave Duluth. That person or those persons will be found. The police excel at such routine. When they do, opportunity will be added to motive. But we still need the means, do we not?"

No one said anything.

Tina said, "Harry?"

I opened my desk drawer and took out a plastic evidence bag containing my wood-handled stiletto. I then walked to Tina's desk and held it up for all to see.

Tina said, "As you can see, we have found the murder weapon. The police are waiting for the forensic report on fingerprints and if the blood matches that of Deloris Anderson."

Kelly Cook slowly stood. "No. It's not possible."

"Miss Cook, the police are most efficient when performing their routine. Once they knew what to look for, it was only a matter of time before they found it."

Suddenly Kelly turned, pulled a pepper spray gun out of her purse and blasted Sergeant Nelson who had moved to block the door. Nelson yelled and clutched her face. Kelly was out the door and Cal was after her, but he didn't have to go far. In our waiting room, Kelly Cook was lying sprawled on the floor, along with Mrs. Bea Wright.

XI – Wednesday, 15 January

BEA HAD THROWN HERSELF, at knee level, into the path of the fleeing Kelly Cook, allowing Cal to apprehend the suspect. He then called for backup and took the whole crew downtown.

On the strength of Tina's bluff, the group confessed to the murders of Deloris Anderson and Jazmin Washington. Tina had pretty much guessed how the whole thing happened. Ashley maintained she had nothing to do with it. Meribeth had worked with Kelly, Robyn, Linda, and Stephanie. Brent didn't know, although he had suspicions as to what happened. He will probably not end up being charged.

The Minneapolis police are working with the Conyers, Georgia authorities to get legitimate copies of a certain company's mail order records to legally establish the sale of the stiletto to Kelly Cook.

On this chilly Wednesday morning, Tina is sitting at her desk. A cigar, a La Gloria Cubana, is perfuming the air. A glass of madeira, not the 1952 Malmsey, sits next to the ashtray. What she's saving the vintage Malmsey for, I don't know. Maybe to celebrate when she retires. Bea, ribs quite sore, is at her desk in the reception area. And I, your faithful reporter, am making sure our expenses are in order. Tina wants as much of the city's four thousand as she can get.

Murder is never easy. And to be honest, this case was a doozy. I take a bit of pride in that I was the one who suggested everyone was in on the murder. Well, everyone connected with Ashley and Morgan. But perhaps the worst thing about murder is there are always those left behind who must pick up the pieces and move on. Unfortunately for Deloris Anderson, there was no one. Perhaps because of that and the fact Bea only has love munchies and isn't pregnant, Bea adopted Deloris's little affenpinscher.

Right now there is open war between little Buddy and Prudy, Manley, and Isis. He does hold his own fairly well, even though outnumbered three to one. Tina isn't happy about our newest family member and maybe that's why the 1952 stays corked. I have a feeling, though, she'll get over it.

From Me to You

I hope you enjoyed *Trio in Death-Sharp Minor*. If you did, please leave a review where you bought the book and on your favorite social media sites. Your review is like word of mouth advertising. And it is pure gold.

Become one of my VIP Readers! You'll get a free copy of *Vampire House and Other Early Cases of Justinia Wright, P.I.* and join the exciting and delicious world of Justinia Wright! You'll get curated and exclusive content, news, and other good stuff.

Sign up today for your free book at BookFunnel! Just click, tap, or scan the QR code!

Continue the Adventure!

If you enjoyed *Trio in Death-Sharp Minor*, Tina and Harry's adventures continue in *But Jesus Never Wept*. Tina must avenge the murder of her client, until she runs into some bad elements from her past. Will her sense of justice prevail?

Click, tap, or scan the QR code to find out!

Also by CW Hawes

I'm a multi-genre author, because more genres means more fun!

I currently have books in the mystery, horror/weird/paranormal, post-apocalyptic, and alternative history/dieselpunk genres.

Please take a look at the My Books page on my website to see all the worlds I inhabit and write about.

Just click, scan, or tap the QR code!

About CW Hawes

CW Hawes is a playwright, award winning poet, and fictioneer. He is also the author of the bestselling *Death Wears a Crimson Hat*.

His interests are wide ranging and this is reflected in both the genres and the contents of his books.

Among CW's many interests are a love for fine food, tea, music (classical, swing, folk, and '50s and '60s pop), philosophy and mythology, art and architecture, books, history, nature, writing instruments (especially pencils, fountain pens, and dip pens), airships, and steam power technology. All of these find a place in his writing.

You can visit him at his website. Just click, tap, or scan the QR code.